MARIE-HÉLÈNE LAFON is an award-winning French writer. Her first novel, *Le Soir du Chien*, won the Renaudot des Lycéens in 2001. Her short story collection *Histoires* was awarded the Goncourt de la Nouvelle in 2016. 'Alphonse', from this collection, was published in English by Granta Magazine in 2020. *Histoire du Fils*, now in English translation as *The Son's Story*, was the winner of the Prix Renaudot, one of France's most prestigious literary prizes. She lives in Paris where she teaches classics.

STEPHANIE SMEE left a career in law to work as a literary translator. Her recent translations include *On the Line: Notes from a Factory* by Joseph Ponthus, shortlisted for the NSW Premier's Translation Prize, and Hannelore Cayre's *The Godmother*, winner of the CWA Crime Fiction in Translation Dagger. She lives in Sydney.

'A work of the purest literary quality: muscular and densely packed, yet graceful in all its movements, and glowing with brilliant detail'
Helen Garner, author of *This House of Grief*

'This took my breath away, again and again. Lafon is magic. She takes us into the hearts of her characters so quickly and so intimately that we see them as they see each other, and feel with them the devastations, desires, longings, secrets and loves that shape the family over generations. A thrilling read in Stephanie Smee's masterful translation'
Anna Funder, *Sunday Times* bestselling author of *Wifedom*

'A magnificent novel'
La Croix

'[Lafon] breathes life into language . . . pure and rich'
Le Monde

'Captivating and heartbreaking from beginning to end . . . each word is chosen with infinite delicacy'
Le Figaro Magazine

'A wonderful novel'
L'Humanité

Marie-Hélène Lafon

THE SON'S STORY

Translated from the French by
Stephanie Smee

MLP

First published in France as *Histoire du Fils*
in 2020 by Buchet/Chastel

First published in paperback in 2024 by Mountain Leopard Press
An imprint of HEADLINE PUBLISHING GROUP

1

Cataloguing in Publication Data is available from the British Library

ISBN 978 1 0354 2023 0

Typeset in Sabon LT by CC Book Production

Printed and bound in Great Britain by Clays Ltd, Elcograf S.p.A.

MIX
Paper | Supporting
responsible forestry
FSC® C104740
www.fsc.org

This book is supported by the Institut français (Royaume-Uni)
as part of the Burgess programme

INSTITUT
FRANÇAIS
Royaume-Uni

HEADLINE PUBLISHING GROUP
An Hachette UK Company
Carmelite House
50 Victoria Embankment
London EC4Y 0DZ

www.headline.co.uk
www.hachette.co.uk

For Jacques,

For Bernadette, in memoriam

"Language is our earth, our flesh. I always think of a project as akin to an excavation, an opening in the earth, and the development of a text, its progression, like a hike in the mountains."

VALÈRE NOVARINA
interview discussing *L'Animal imaginaire*, 2019

Thursday, 25 April 1908

ARMAND'S BARE FEET slide over the parquetry floor; he does not want to wake Paul who is still asleep and making that disgusting little sound he makes with his lips, like a puppy suckling at its mother's teat. He will wait a little, but not too long, Paul must not wake up, he would spoil the fun of the reunion, Paul spoils everything. They were born on the same day, he and Paul, on 2 August 1903; he knows, from his mother and his aunt, that there had never previously been any twins in the two families. He would rather not be a twin or, at least, would have preferred Georges and not Paul. He knows that is impossible, because things are what they are, Aunt Marguerite is always saying that, he turns the words over and over in his mouth, feeling them against his teeth, this odd phrase that slips away, escapes from him, and he stops for a moment to ponder the grey expressions of his Aunt Marguerite, her sayings and her smell, cold ashes and cured sausage. He often stops to think about the smells and colours of people, of things, of rooms

3

and moments, and when Antoinette used to live with them in Chanterelle, he would make her laugh with what she called his whimsies, how she would laugh and laugh, she would weep too from the corners of her eyes, she would be laughing so hard; now there is nobody to share his whimsies with anymore. Georges smells of plum jam, when his aunt lets it simmer away in the copper basin in the summertime, he smells like that jam at precisely that moment, not when it is spread on bread for afternoon tea in the winter; even his father eats it and compliments his aunt who does not reply but looks at his father as if seeing him for the first time. Amélie smells of the river, swollen with snow melt in the springtime. Paul smells of the wind and of the cold blades of the kitchen knives they are forbidden to touch. As for his mother, he hesitates, it is always different, the snow as it turns blue in the evening at the edge of the woods, fresh coffee. There are times too she smells red. And for his father, vegetable soup perhaps, but that is not quite it, he stops, something congeals within him and he would rather not go on. The smells are a game, and his father is not to be toyed with. Georges' little room, between their parents' room and his own that he shares with his brother, smells of the white heat of the flat-irons that his mother or Amélie glide over the linen, bending an arm then extending an elbow, his mother's right arm and elbow, for Amélie her left, even though she is the more deft of the two. The big bath on a Saturday evening, with the warm, soft towels, and his mother and aunt bent over him, over them, the big bath smells pink; Antoinette and Amélie do not help out with the bath on Saturdays. His aunt says – separating every word – tea-towels and serviettes are not to be mixed; or move one's feet, lose one's seat, or he who sleeps forgets his hunger, or sow the wind and reap the storm, or the apple does not fall far from the tree. He knows every one of his aunt's sayings by heart, especially those he does not understand, and sometimes he recites them, silently, word for word, to put himself to sleep, or to calm himself, to settle down, like now, when he feels he would like to leap down the six steps of the staircase in a single bound and land in the kitchen, on Antoinette's shoulder, like a swallow. His aunt also says that one swallow does not a summer make. He does his best to be patient, just until the dining room clock strikes the half hour, so he tries hard to think about strawberries, the ones Antoinette will have picked for him at Embort, the first of the season, and about the ones from his aunt's garden. He knows his mother, his aunt and Amélie are in the kitchen preparing the laundry, it will start today and last two whole days. Antoinette will come too, she comes back for the larger household chores, she is probably already here, she promised him the first strawberries and Antoinette always keeps her word. She no longer lives in Chanterelle, she lives in Embort, he has not forgotten the name, much milder country where big cherry trees grow, she tells him about it and rounding her two arms describes how the cherry trees grow in the orchards in this new part of the world where she lives with her husband. He cried a lot when she left with her curly-haired husband, even though his mother and Aunt Marguerite explained that it was normal, that young women like Antoinette, when they find a husband, leave the children they are looking after in other people's houses to follow their husband and live with him in a house of their own where they will have their own children. Aunt Marguerite had bowed her head as she spoke these words and he had understood not to ask further questions. He knows Aunt Marguerite has neither husband, nor house, nor children, and he can sense the sadness that seeps from her skin and gives her a particular odour which is neither that of his mother, nor of Antoinette or Amélie. It is a grey, cold scent that grips his stomach; he could cry, but he does not, he must not, he would be mocked. He leaves his bedroom, the window at the end of the corridor is filled with light, like the big stained-glass window in the church on a bright day; the sun comes up on this side and nobody ever closes the shutters on that window, not even in winter. He is alone in the corridor, everybody is downstairs, in the kitchen, and his father has left for the council chambers at the Mairie, on Thursday mornings his father heads off very early to the Mairie. He was still in bed when he heard him close the door and walk across the square; when he listens, with his eyes closed, because he hears better with his eyes closed, he can recognise their step and the particular way they each have of doing things, his mother, his aunt, his father, Paul, Georges, Amélie and even other people, like Solange or Antonin, who come to help but who do not live with them; he can pick out the bark of each dog in the village, too, it is his game and his secret, Paul must not know. Armand takes a few steps forward, he walks into the warm light, he can feel it, on his feet, on his hands, his face, his hair, he closes his eyes. Later on, soon, when he is old enough, he will be a choir boy, it is what his mother and aunt will want, his father will not be able to stop it, he has heard Antoinette say as much to Amélie even if they did change the subject when he came into the kitchen. Antoinette and Amélie are afraid of his father, everybody is afraid of him, even Paul, his father's fury is like a thunderstorm, the house trembles, the earth trembles, the day grows dark as night; when it is over, when his father leaves, they can start to breathe again. But in the meantime, they can always recite to themselves the prayer said for him and Paul by their mother in the evening in their bedroom; Georges does not understand, he is still too little. Armand tried when his father was last raging, but it did not work, and he knows why, the prayer starts with Our Father, and the words stick in his craw, he cannot get them out. It would be good to talk to Antoinette about it today, or tomorrow; after that she will be gone again, as soon as the laundry is finished, and he does not know when she will be back. Antoinette has her ideas, a solution for everything, she can do magic tricks, he loves her arms, her hair, her neck, he loves to duck quickly into the empty church with her on a sunny afternoon, just to make a genuflection and the sign of the cross in the puddles of yellow-reddish light that splash through the big stained glass window. They sit for a moment, too, in the confessional, each on their own side, she to the right he to the left, the wood is soft and gleaming, the confessional smells of wax, of honey, of fresh butter. He loves church, he is going to be a choir boy, he loves Antoinette.

He hears her voice rising from the kitchen, mixed with his mother's, his aunt and Amélie are not saying anything. He stands there on the top step, he waits, he knows that his mother and aunt have already been up for a long time and have put on the water to heat over the great stove in two very large stock pots that are only used for the laundry; the rest of the time they are kept on the bottom shelf in the wash room where he and Georges love to play with the deepest one which is big enough to allow Georges to slip into it completely. He disappears inside, as if into a sort of rigid casing, and tips backwards and forwards or left to right, imitating the chickens after they have laid, and the pot looks like it is clucking and dancing and the boys laugh, unable to stop. They do it when nobody is looking, when the grown-ups are distracted, they would be scolded because cooking utensils must not be damaged. Paul thinks it is a baby's game and he makes fun of them but does not tell. Armand takes two steps down the stairs and sits on the third where, without being seen, he can watch what is happening. Antoinette is here; she is bustling about, arms full of washing, her short crop of curly hair is red, Antoinette is a redhead, not ginger, he does not like the word that his father sometimes uses. Antoinette's hair is red like the fox that he and his mother saw last winter as they crossed the big upper field one snowy evening. His mother had squeezed his hand which she had been holding in hers, they had stopped, the fox too, all three of them rooted to the spot; then the creature had been swallowed up by the wood, only its tracks had remained, barely visible on the hard, blue snow. Antoinette is a miracle, like the fox. His father kills foxes, his father is a hunter, but soon, though, he is to be a choir boy and he will not hunt, he does not want to kill animals, not magical foxes, nor velvety hares, nor leaping deer, nor birds, not any sort of bird, especially not birds. Everything is all jumbled up inside, the birds, Antoinette the fox, the stained glass in the church, the strawberries, the fresh butter of the confessional, the secret of the big stock pot. He does not try to resist, it is all too much to gulp down in a single mouthful, his bare feet silently tap the fourth step, beating time to his delight, he would like to take flight. He likes to remember last summer, when he did not yet know Antoinette would leave, they would go, in the evening, the two of them, they would water the lettuces, especially the lettuces, and other vegetables that did not much interest him, but he liked to carry the little jugs, the blue one and the white, he would

9

follow Antoinette, he would breathe her in with the smell of the damp earth, he had wings, he would gallop from the well to the other end of the garden, careful not to ruin anything, fetching water, and more water still. The garden was a kingdom of green and gold, the garden was the whole world and the light was unending. Then, before heading back in, they would stop by the strawberry patch, they would be crouched down, facing each other, on either side of the garden bed, and they would fossick gently among the fresh lacework of leaves, feeling with their fingers the swelling strawberries, just three or four, no more, so as not to upset his aunt. Soon there would be another summer, but Antoinette would no longer be there. The chimes of half past eight leap out, and he can no longer contain himself, he is standing up now, his feet are bare on the top steps. Antoinette has her back to him, she is at the stove, she has not yet seen him, but he knows she is waiting for him, he is in the air, he shoots forward, he runs, he throws himself around the legs of his Antoinette just as she turns; she has lifted the scalding, deep stock pot from the stove, she is carrying it, clutching it, arms outstretched, and it ends in a scream that rents the air and wakens Paul.

Thursday, 23 January 1919

IT WAS PREP TIME and they were supposed to be studying. He rubbed his feet under the desk, one against the other; his feet were always cold, even though his mother used to tuck into his suitcase pairs of fine woollen grey or black slipper-socks that she would knit for him during the winter, high up there in Chanterelle. In the mornings, in the dormitory, he would discreetly slip them on under his socks, they fitted him perfectly, and were soft against his skin. Nobody could know, at the *lycée*, that Paul Lachalme worried about having cold feet and wore slipper-socks knitted by his mother. He had a reputation to maintain. There was a handful of them, four or five, who had continued to follow his lead all last year and joined him to claim, proclaim and declaim that they were sixteen years old, finally, and they were ready to sign up, or try to at least, they were keen to head off, to leave this shameful pathetic backwater where women, and children, the elderly, the halt and the lame, the weaklings and pen-pushers were all waiting, as the everyday

13

banality of their peaceful existence grew along with the size of their bellies, while elsewhere men were living, and dying, on top of each other. Paul was fond of his way with words, the way he could string a sentence together; he had a taste for it, some said a talent for it, and he was happy to put his skills to good use in the heated discussions between boarders on the burning topic of this never-ending war. Those who wanted to leave, and join forces with, or replace, or avenge fathers, uncles, brothers, cousins and friends, imposed their views on the others; boys hardly dared think, let alone say, that they might be afraid, or that this war bogged down in the mud for the last four years no longer had any real point, or that they did not know how they could inflict it, this departure, on top of everything else, on a mother, or a sister already destined to wear black and doomed to tears. The Armistice had cut to the point and put paid to the procrastination and chest-beating. Two months later, an interminable January was stretching into the icy grey of the weeks for which they would all be crammed together until the distant Easter break, and Paul Lachalme's feet were cold as he studied in the evening. They had been sent back to childhood, they would not be heroes, they would not be killed in action, it was too late for any of it; they were dependent, they were once again powerless, they had never been anything else, they submitted and struggled with it all, the weeks, the cold feet, the first *Eclogue* and other necessary educational evils. *Sub tegmine fagi*, beneath a spreading beech tree; it could not come fast enough, Easter, beneath the beech trees, in Chanterelle, in April, when the world is in spring; another set expression; not exactly. Paul shakes his head. He says nothing to anyone about the high country, nor about Chanterelle, his parents, or his aunt; it's his kingdom, not for sharing, and he cannot risk any display of weakness to the army of mocking Aurillac boys who wear their rural origins less obviously than he and his brother, and who are swift to sink their fangs into anyone who outdoes them in anything. And he and Georges outdo them in everything, that's just the size of it, it's glaringly obvious, but you can't afford ever to slacken off, nor let down your guard. He is Paul Lachalme, and he never lets down his guard, even if his feet are cold. *Sub tegmine fagi; fagi,* from *fagus,* from which we have *Fagus sylvatica* or beech; that much he's happy enough to have learned, studying Virgil isn't a complete waste of time, nor is his teacher, Michon; they call him Père Michon, two capitals, because of his monkish baldness, or PM, just like the English; he hails from Guéret and can reel off the *Eclogues* in juicy, impeccable chunks with an emotion that is almost infectious. Paul and Georges love giving their mother and aunt a bit of a Latin lesson; they never studied it themselves but they have a fondness for the language because they hear it in church. Paul suspects they have a vision of him and Georges crowned in halos of intangible mystery and knowledge, and that they love them for it all the more, if that is possible. He would almost begrudge his brother the gleaming Greek origins of his first name, Geórgios, the farm labourer, but for the fact that he would give even more to be called André ever since Père Michon casually mentioned its masculine etymology, as if throwing the class a bone. André means the man who gets hard; those had not been PM's precise words, he had respected conventions, but they had understood, and he knew that they had understood, that some of them, at least, had picked up the smooth hint and would remember. Paul would like to give himself a shake; still a good half hour of prep to go; he shifts his feet under the desk, wriggles his toes in their woollen under-socks, feels Mourot the invigilator's glacial eyes slide over him, across his forehead, over his skull, down his back, he's a nasty piece of work, waiting to ambush you, full of rat-cunning, not to be trusted. Another one who can't get it up. Besides, his name's Camille, a girl's name. Paul spends a moment thinking about first names, he lets his mind wander, killing time. *Sub tegmine fagi*, roll on Easter, so he can be back in Chanterelle; the beeches up there, they're something else compared to the ones in Virgil, something else again to the neatly pruned chestnut trees in the big quadrangle of the lycée in Aurillac, down on the plains. In Chanterelle, once he had handled the obstacle of his father, he would be fussed over by his mother and aunt, and there would be girls; girls to see, to sniff, to smell, from a distance. High country girls were not to be touched, it would get around in no time; you had to be content just to look, from a distance, but it was still better than here, at school, where you could have your tongue hanging out, salivating, for weeks, without there ever being a single thing you could sink your teeth into. Up there, the girls would wander through the square in chirping huddles, they wouldn't go on their own to the café, and definitely not to the restaurant or hotel, but back home, when he stood at his bedroom window, it was like having a seat in the dress circle, completely discreet, and he wouldn't miss a thing, especially in summer, which was high season for his girl-cousins, and for their female friends.

Mourot is patrolling the rows, he doesn't smell good. Paul hesitates, rancid butter leeks vinaigrette old soup, the lingering stench of food, the mark of a mean life, recooked and reheated. Mourot plants himself squarely next to him, legs apart, sagging slightly at the knees, hands behind his back, fingers loosely entwined, palms open; his nails are not clean and the almost-tender pink of his palms bothers Paul Lachalme, who averts his eyes, battens down the hatches, and would prefer to focus on reciting his Virgil while he waits for the evening bell. He ponders his *Eclogue* listlessly, he knows it, chews it over like a piece of old tobacco, he drifts. Four rows ahead, the angled nape of his brother's neck belies his intense concentration. Georges excels in everything and is not reluctant to make an effort in those few areas where he will not triumph without it. The lycée fairly hums with his numerous exploits, in French composition, in translation from Greek and Latin, in Greek prose composition, and even in mathematics, a barbaric subject that he, Paul, openly scorns. As the eldest, he could take umbrage at Georges' brilliance, were his manifest upper hand over his younger brother not based on intangible and firmly entrenched family custom. People know they are twisted like rope, tied together, that they've come down from the far north of the *département*, steep, surly country caparisoned with interminable snows from November to April, and streaked by imperious storms for the two tumultuous summer months when every self-respecting farming property in the département's south sends their plentiful herds of red cattle up beyond the peaks of Le Puy Mary and Le Lioran, to the plateaux of Le Cézallier and Le Limon, where the animals enjoy the heady delight of grazing on mountains blanketed in lush grass. Locals from that *préfecture* and its immediate surrounds readily give people the once over if they are down from either Allanche, Condat, Murat or Riom-ès-Montagnes, one of the four high country cantons, calling them *gabatches* – savages in other words. The word is spat out, syllables snatched, rarely written, even if those from the lower parts can never quite cast off a sort of mute admiration, mingled with fear, for the prized characteristics of endurance, tenacity, doggedness even, said to be in generous supply among the rough-edged locals from the high country. Paul and Georges Lachalme escaped in part from this subtle appraisal, less on account of their provenance – people were more or less aware that they were the sons of a prosperous innkeeper heavily involved in local politics, and the grandsons of farmers – than as a result of some unspoken charm that seemed to attach to their very being. It could be seen in their joints, their shoulders wrists ankles, at once strong yet fine, in their complexion, pale but nonetheless vigorous, in their hair, soft and thick, an almost nondescript golden brown, always groomed but never ostentatiously so, in their clear gaze of changing blues and greys. Their teeth were perfect, and their figures already long, feline and powerful. Nor did they consider it beneath them to excel in sport; everything about them was bursting with a grace, a self-evidence that was, by turn, striking, seductive, coaxing and irritating. Georges kept quiet under the wing of Paul, who had a way with words and who would exploit that facility with poorly contained rage. The war was over, there would be no sowing of wild oats, he would have preferred to be fired up, to prove himself in some manly fashion, to flatten the enemy, cleave them in two, have their guts for garters, triumph over death itself and collapse on his laurels, strapped into a glorious uniform. He had turned eleven on 2 August 1914, and had been humiliated that his father, already approaching fifty, had not even been mobilised among the rearguard. No man would fly the family colours, his paternal uncles were too old, there was no uncle on his mother's side, not even by marriage; there were only female cousins, four on his father's side, between the ages of thirteen and sixteen, still too young to be either engaged or married and turned into mute and languid widows; there was nobody, well as good as nobody; only the farmers' eldest son and nephew had been called up, had headed off. He knew them, certainly; he had always seen them without seeing them, stocky and shortish, busy in the local area, impressive when it came to their work, but they were not of his blood and, despite a persistence of prayers on the part of his mother and aunt, they did not excite the dreams of Paul Lachalme. The nephew had been declared missing in action since November 1917; the son had returned, listless and gassed; Paul had caught a glimpse of him over the Christmas holidays, slumped in a woman's armchair in front of the hearth; his mother had been weeping, his father had said nothing, their son was scarcely able to speak, forever averting his gaze and spitting up reddish threads which he would collect with slow gestures in a permanently soiled handkerchief. Paul had been ashamed and frightened. It would have been better to die; he had thought it, but had not said it, not even to his mother or his aunt who he knew, however, were attuned, to his every inner turmoil. The future had suddenly emptied out. Virgil, the shade offered by the beeches, evening prep and tedious weeks of boarding school were his whole horizon, for at least another two years. Waiting, waiting. His feet were cold and he too smelled, not like Mourot, but it was a strong smell, and it wasn't good. He sniffed himself, he was fermenting. The only things left were women, their female bodies; he would say the word "females" surreptitiously, he liked the wolfish tremor of the word; so then, females, and everything they were hiding, tightly held beneath their blouses and between their knees. He would inhale that scent, that's what he wanted. He was ready for the great hunt, his weapons were polished. He and the lads would talk about it amongst themselves, using crude words. He knew the actions, knew his juice. There was an agitation among the males in the recesses of the boarding school. The previous summer in Condat at the Saint's Day ball, he had been unstoppable on the dance floor, insatiable, he had had some luck with a tall girl; she had been forward and cheerful, fresh from Clermont where people were probably a little more open-minded. This Clarisse – a grandma's name despite her twenty years – had followed him, perhaps even preceded him, down to the banks of the river Rhue. He had seen, he had touched, nibbled, nudged with his snout, his tongue, his teeth; her thighs were silken, Clarisse was panting, stretched out on the damp grass. But he had not finished it off, she had slipped through his fingers, without his quite understanding how or why. She had vanished, the slippery Clarisse. He had returned to Chanterelle, enraged. He almost envied his brother whom he sensed to be some way off from this stormy territory, stifled still by his childish state. Women were off limits, at least the girls in his circle, guarded like reliquaries, cossetted by alarmed mothers, repellent aunts and prickly principles. Moreover you could like girls, fall in love with them; he was working that out, that delicious relinquishment, that heady vertigo, he had read a bit and knew Victor Hugo's "Rose" by heart. The love potion was bitter, he would not be defeated, not chained up, not like that, no such definitive poison would flow through his blood. He had no desire for pain, he wanted flesh. That word, though, had too much of a whiff of Mass about it; the word he thought and used was meat, and sometimes his hands would tremble under the sheets.

The second fortnight of January was harsh, the ice had to be broken every morning in the long room with the washbasins, ablutions ended up abbreviated as a result and Paul did not like this rancid odour that seeped out from under his arms. At home, his mother and aunt had given him a habit of and a taste for hot baths. Every Friday evening, at around five o'clock, in the absence of his father who found such fanciful notions irritating, and without resorting to Suzanne, the young maid who had entered into service with the family in the same year he had turned ten, they would fuss over him, testing the water's temperature with an expert hand, disappearing opportunely just as he emerged, streaming and stark naked, straddling the tub with a strapping leg to wrap himself in the enormous monogrammed piqué cotton towel, which his mother would have spread out beforehand on the back of the nearest chair. The ceremony took place in a corner of the large kitchen which would be screened off for the occasion behind stretched paper patterned with grey foliage. The water would have been warming on the stove since morning in the two deep stock pots reserved for that purpose and for the laundry on wash days. Georges, who was speedier and more accommodating, would then wash in the lukewarm leftovers of his brother's bath. In summer, they would happily bathe in the Santoire, their blood whipped by its bracing, wilful waters which, in a certain shady water hole they had christened Hell's sinkhole, retained its restorative coolness even in the heat of the most searing days. On Sunday, 26 January, Paul declared that he would be giving himself a proper wash, even if it meant using barely melted ice. Swaggering, he kept his word, teeth gritted, alone in the long room deserted by his friends who were less vigilant about their hygiene. Two days later, ears humming, throat on fire, sweating, coughing and struggling for breath, he was dispatched unceremoniously to the infirmary where a young doctor from town, who had been urgently summoned, expressed alarm at the state of his bronchial tubes. There was no family history of weak chests, Paul would have assured him of that, had he had the strength; but, with no voice and trembling legs, he found himself consigned to one of the two rooms furnished with a single bed that were reserved for very ill patients and there he was delivered into the expert hands of the nurse who cinched him tight beneath three blankets and a firmly drawn blue sheet, addressed him formally and called him "young man" in a voice at once commanding and captivating. He was on the point of fainting, unable to offer any further resistance, and only realised the following evening that there was a new nurse. Generations of boys at the lycée had dreaded the brisk Madame Brégançon, a massive and ageless matron, bound into an immaculate blouse stretched taut over her drooping and dissuasive outline. No boarder, going all the way back to the Stone Age, would have dreamed to scrounge for the slightest substitute of maternal, even feminine, solicitude from the unsinkable Madame Brégançon. Nothing was known of her, she was barely even ridiculed, and she had obviously taken her leave of the place with no fuss and not a sound. Mademoiselle G. Léoty was her replacement. Paul liked the name, embroidered on to her blouse, even if he found the initial somewhat distracting. Georgette, Gisèle, Gertrude, Gilberte, Ginette – he was foundering in a marshland of first names, but the surname had flair, a degree of seriousness, and a fervent, elegant resonance that conjured up a certain image. Feverish and listless, he thought about ships, about thrushes on the wing too, about the first biting mornings of autumn that herald the start to the auspicious days of the hunting season. He became attentive to the voice, grave veiled shimmering velvety warm. He exhausted his adjectives. He applied himself to the matter, eyes closed, rambling and coiled within his skin. Grainy, perhaps, Mademoiselle Léoty's voice was grainy, but not grating, nor rasping; tender; no, not tender, the opposite, almost the very opposite, it passed over you, through you, burrowed into you, reached within you, under your skin. On the third day, the Wednesday, he settled on warm and grainy, and he knew the precise extent to which it was also erotic. Over the following days, he tried to drag things out. The grey January was dwindling; his brother, his sole permitted visitor, was tasked with spreading alarming rumours as to the contagious nature of his condition in order to discourage the more adventurous members of his inner circle who were fomenting a clandestine, nocturnal incursion. Paul wanted things to remain behind closed doors; the situation was critical; beating away beneath Mademoiselle Léoty's white uniform was the Holy Grail, that would do. He supposed her to be about thirty; her face was stern and her mouth already pursed, but her ears were perfect, her eyes bright, her neck supple, her nape cool, and he suspected a luxuriousness to the brown hair gathered in a chignon beneath the thin regulation cap. All of it heralded certain delights. He was not at all surprised by the very sure instinct that spared him the doubt and procrastinations normally associated with such beginnings. He knew he was handsome, he was hungry, he was young, and this woman, who was no longer exactly young herself, recognised that in him. He felt it, he had felt it, since Thursday; when she had checked on him in the evening, she had neither blushed nor averted her gaze when, seated on the edge of the bed in his blue pyjamas, waiting for her to appear, he had made a move towards her in a state of manifest tumescence, on the pretext of testing the new-found steadiness of his gait. He was wobbling, she had taken him by the shoulders, they were the same height. She had directed the intense brilliance of her clear eyes upon him, and she had said, in a voice verging on laughter, get back into bed young man it's difficult to feel steady on three legs.

Saturday, 19 August 1950

ANDRÉ HAD ALWAYS HAD two words for his mothers. It was a bit difficult to explain. He would use *maman* for Hélène, his aunt, who had raised him in Figeac, and for Gabrielle, his mother, who lived in Paris, he reserved the more formal *ma mère*; he had not spent more than four weeks a year with her for the first seventeen years of his life, and even fewer now that he no longer lived in his childhood home. Juliette had already been introduced to Hélène and Léon; he had done so in the spring of 1949, less than a year after they had met for the first time, when he had been certain; even if, in some ways, he had been certain from the beginning, from the moment he had seen Juliette, even before he had spoken to her. He liked to think of that, how he had known immediately, about Juliette, then and forever. In the maquis, he had been with a woman who had been older than he was, a refugee from the north who might have been Jewish, who had been married in another life and had said to call her Silvia. They had wanted to ask her questions but nobody dared. Once, she had asked him his age, his real age, and had told him he looked a lot like her brother, except younger; she had had no news of him since October 1940. He had thought, without saying so, that it was perhaps a dubious criterion by which to choose a lover from a group of males, all of them starving, more or less, and honed by the desire to live beyond themselves, out on the prow. That is what she would say, this woman, Silvia, to live out on the prow, to be honed; she would often use images which were not at once evident, but they would graft onto one's bones and there they would remain. They were still there, the one about the prow, and others; they would surface at moments when he least expected it and he would not resist, he would yield, allow it to happen, he was faithful. Silvia had also told him that his name, André, came from a Greek word meaning man in the virile, male sense, as opposed to man in its general meaning, human beings, men and women, mixed together; mixed up, she would add, and she would laugh. She laughed a lot, she laughed too much, she laughed savagely, catastrophically, she used to say, too; a savage or catastrophic laugh. There was something of the teacher about her, even in her laugh. She knew Latin and classical Greek. She had been his first woman, his only one before Juliette, more or less. He had not mentioned Silvia to Juliette. Like everybody, Juliette had known about the maquis. When, after the war, Pierre had gone back to his job at the factory, he had been running the show. Management, who had continued quietly to work first with Vichy and then for the Germans, could refuse nothing to a hero of Free France. He had made sure they were taken on, all three of them, Christian, Yves and André, because he knew them, knew what they were capable of, and also because he knew the war had snatched them in full flight from their youth, prevented them studying, from taking on an apprenticeship. In the autumn of 1945 there had been nothing for it but to find a job, to earn a living. Pierre was almost twice their age, he might have been their father and, in a way, that is what he had become, for him especially. André would have liked to choose him as his best man, but he had not dared, Christian and Yves would not have understood, it would have created an awkwardness between them, Pierre was their boss too, he was boss to all three of them; but they had a father, Christian and Yves, he did not, not one like theirs in any event. André disliked entertaining such thoughts, so he kept them to himself and did not voice them, except to Juliette. She understood that one day he would try to find out; it would have meant asking Gabrielle who had never said anything; but there was no speaking to Gabrielle, not even Hélène could do that, and André even less so. Everything slid off Gabrielle. She was neither hostile, nor aloof, but she eluded you, there was no knowing how to reach her. And yet to see her embrace her sister, her Hélène her Lélou her *alouette*, when she would arrive at the station at Figeac, and when she would leave again. Her eyes would be closed, and so often, caught in her enfolding embrace, she would just keep on hugging her; all about them, on the platform, people would wait. Gabrielle was older, by barely a year. The sisters bore no resemblance to each other, apart from their voice; there was nothing about them physically, nor in their gestures, but their voices were the same, although there was something almost serious, veiled, in Hélène's voice, something more enveloping and tender than in Gabrielle's. Their intonation, their inflections were so similar that Léon and the cousins would sometimes mistake them, when one of them would toss off a remark, from one room to another, especially if Gabrielle had been back for several days and had become part of the furniture. André never mistook them and, as far as he was concerned, Gabrielle never became part of the furniture; that was Hélène's expression, one she reserved exclusively for her sister. Gabrielle had her own space at 8 rue Bergandine where she would spend four weeks each year, one at Christmas, and three in August. She would sleep upstairs, in the green room, which everybody used to call Gaby's room. Hélène would fetch her from the five o'clock train with André, and the girls, his cousins, would come, and Léon too if he were not at the shop. Gabrielle would step off the train *en Parisienne*, wearing hat, gloves, elegant shoes, a tailored ensemble, smart luggage, just a hint of something hard about the set of her posture, and she would depart again similarly decked out. The metamorphosis would happen with all the hugging, on the platform;

something within her would expand. Relaxed, loosened, she would bend down, Hélène at her side; she would kiss André, three times, calling him Dadou, as did everyone else. Later, that evening, or the following day, she would say to him, as her eyes brushed lightly over him, and she took his right wrist in her dry, warm hand, that he had grown, that he was handsome, more and more handsome, and that she was so proud. Hélène and Gabrielle had always been joined at the hip; it came from the childhood they had experienced, the two of them, like surviving a harsh landscape; they almost never spoke of it, but it was understood. Three older brothers, two of whom had been killed at the Somme, a father too young at his death when Hélène had been only seventeen, a worn-out mother who had also departed prematurely, before the birth of André's cousins, the girls, an out-of-the-way farm, somewhere high above Gramat, on the plateaux, three cows, some scree some goats some sheep; the surviving brother, whom they did not see, still lived there, a forsaken old bachelor. Hélène and Gabrielle liked the plains, the lower, more mellow country, and the conveniences of town. Gabrielle had left for Aurillac and then for Paris, where he, André, had been born, when she was almost thirty-seven. Hélène had been by her side and had spent four weeks in Paris where she had disliked everything, the small, cramped lodgings, the pace, the relentless grey, the damp February cold when, in the Lot, spring was already making an appearance, primroses were flowering around the house and grandfather *pépé* was already preparing to turn the soil in the garden. She had particularly disliked what her instincts as a gentle and decent woman suspected to be the harsher, cordoned-off aspects of her sister's life. Back in Figeac, Léon and his parents, *pépé* and *mémé*, looked after the three girls who were champing at the bit, impatient to have their mother return with this late-in-the-day cousin whom they would keep, whom they would raise for as long as Gabrielle's circumstances remained to be regularised. That was *mémé*'s word, *regularised*, the grandmother who loved her only daughter-in-law, the heaven-sent Hélène, her joy, her peace, the mother of her three granddaughters, *mémé* who loved her enough to adopt the elder sister, too, this horse who had bolted and who had worked first as a nurse in Aurillac, and was now working in Paris, as what exactly it was unclear, and who had ended up contracting a child, a boy, with no father. It was always better if it was a boy when there was no father around; *mémé*, who was never called anything else, must also have thought it was no example for Léon and Hélène's girls, and must also have harboured a few less charitable thoughts. She had probably shared those with her daughter-in-law, for she was unable to keep anything from her, not the good, nor the bad, nor any of the rest; there was no hiding anything from Hélène. And then *mémé* had been like everyone else in the household, which is to say smitten by that little boy, André, who had been surrounded by the boundless love of those five women and two men, not to mention the neighbourhood women in rue Bergandine and, later, every one of his school mistresses. Gabrielle, fortunately enough, had never regularised her circumstances, for it is uncertain how any of them could ever have been separated from the child and allowed him to return, with both mother and father, to Paris. They had held on to their treasure, they had held on to Dadou; when all was said and done, life did sometimes make things right.

Before the war, before he knew Silvia, André too discovered, like everyone else in the household, that life generally did make things right. Even the war, at the outset, had not seemed to him a catastrophe. He could not have said quite why. He had been sixteen in 1940, he had rushed around with everybody else, nobody really had stopped to reflect, they had rallied, people were arriving from every which where and, in June, Gabrielle had appeared. Hélène and Léon found themselves growing in number. *Mémé* had died in May of 1939, a year after *pépé*, and their little house which had remained empty, had been put to use accommodating two sisters from Dormans who had been forced to take to the road with their three children, with no news of their husbands who were either still serving or who had already been taken prisoner. After them a couple of utterly bewildered retirees had been taken in who, with fear in their belly, had fled the suburbs of Reims. It is worse than in 1914, that is what they kept saying, over and over, it is worse than 1914, they would never leave again, never, they would sooner die than be invaded a third time, at their age, nobody would ever force them from their home again, too bad about everything they had left behind in the north. They had stayed, and after ten years they had become indistinguishable from the locals but for the persistent trace of an accent. *Pépé*'s vast vegetable patch had become their kingdom, with Léon disinclined to work on that part of the garden, and they would marvel endlessly at the benevolent and generous climate of a region where they were sorry not to have been born and where they would most certainly die. They would be at the wedding, as would almost the entire neighbourhood, or at least the residents of rue Bergandine who had watched André grow up and were now delighted to see him doing so well, at the age of twenty-six, in a promising position and with a fiancée endowed with such a sunny disposition. The young couple would live in Toulouse where Juliette also worked; they would come back often, it was easy now with the latest cars, women were starting to drive. It was a sight to behold, to see André, Dadou, give his Juliette a lesson in reverse parking, everybody enjoyed that, they did, never had they laughed so hard. Léon, who was such a poor driver himself, had not held back with his voluble, high-handed commentary, and there was André, struggling to keep his temper. People particularly relished the contagious joy which had always been present in that house, such a happy malady in the face of so many unpleasant ones, and this fatherless André had found luck in his misfortune. He had converted the try. He had muddied the Figeac team jersey sufficiently to deserve the rugby ball guard of honour on emerging from the church. It would be a proper celebration, one where ration cards and the relentless end-of-month juggling could be forgotten. In September of 1944, Silvia had disappeared; one morning she had no longer been there. There had been no explanation. Pierre, who must have known, had said nothing and six years later he was still silent. In 1944, André had felt at once helpless and relieved; she had been too much for him, that woman, not too old nor too complicated, simply too much. She ventured places he could not, neither to follow nor precede her, nor even to accompany her; and skin did nothing to change that. He had learned that much, too, with her; that glorious affairs of the flesh and the unspoken trust they suggest do nothing to stave off solitude. The others knew, about him and Silvia. At the start, they had felt that it was fraught, something about it caught; a single woman alone in a group, it was often difficult; and a woman like her, all the more so. Pierre was in charge, and Silvia, in a way, his lieutenant, the word did not exist in the feminine. It fell to Pierre to settle the issue with her, should he deem it necessary. Pierre had not budged, he must have sensed Silvia would know how to behave, how to manage the situation, without placing anybody in danger. He had been vindicated. Then, in the autumn of 1944 and in the months that had followed, André had been so busy rushing from pillar to post with Pierre, Christian, Yves and the others that he had spared scarcely a thought for Silvia, except, from time to time, for a stirring deep within. He had understood he was attached to her in that way too. Until Juliette, he had never really been tempted by other women. Silvia would have said they did not give him an appetite. He had her voice in his ear, her way with words. As time went on he felt that some of her expressions would stay with him, would be a part of him, always, and for the most part, he kept them to himself, because they did not fit with his world, they could not be pigeonholed, they struggled under his skin like creatures caught in a trap, they formed part of his groundwater. André was not fond of gorges, not even the one that gaped open at Padirac less than an hour by car from Figeac, and which was adored by Hélène and Léon and their entire tribe. He did not like those inky waters that carved out ravines in the dark. He had chosen the light the warmth the day the delight. Everybody had liked Juliette, just like that, there had been no need to make an effort, because she was who she was. Hélène and Léon had taken to her, as had his three cousins, the three cousins' three husbands, and the five daughters of the three cousins and their three husbands. The five daughters would be flower girls at the wedding. There was a flurry of dresses sewn, gloves designed and crocheted, bouquets planned, everybody busying themselves on all fronts, everybody deployed, everybody with something to offer. Juliette's younger sister and her mother were also plying the needle in Sarlat. André suspected all of this activity but would not see anything before the fateful day. Juliette would be a freshly minted treasure. The day after the wedding, in the evening, after a six-hour drive, bags still open behind them on the large bed, they had stood on the balcony looking out at the expansive view of green blue ocean. Juliette had wanted the ocean proper, and a hotel in just the right spot, on the shore where the waves broke. They had done their research, they had taken the room for six days, until the next Saturday, they could afford to treat themselves. André had felt the bright warmth of Juliette's blonde shoulder against him, against his right arm. She had blurted out in a rush, as if reciting a poem to the teacher at the front of the class, not looking at him, not breathing, not moving, her body coiled, yesterday your mother told me about your father, his name is Paul Lachalme he was born in 1903 he is forty-seven years old sixteen years younger than she is they met in Aurillac at the boys' lycée he is a lawyer he lives in Paris on boulevard Arago in the fourteenth arrondissement at number 34 he has a house and there is some family property a hotel some land in Chanterelle in the Cantal.

Friday, 17 August 1934

SHE HAS GONE. His mother has gone, the train has taken her away. He likes it better when she isn't there, but he has a feeling that it's not something he should say, nor something he should show, even if you can't hide anything from Hélène. He, André, can hide nothing from Hélène who sees straight through his skin, into his bones, into the tangled folds of his brain. Hélène sees, but she doesn't scold, she doesn't judge, doesn't frown, doesn't raise her voice, doesn't purse her mouth. She gives hugs, she takes you on her knee, she doesn't use a lot of words. She'll make a cake, you can go to the garden with her to pick warm strawberries or furry raspberries, she strokes the nape of your neck at your hairline. He doesn't understand how Gabrielle and Hélène can be sisters, and daughters of the same father and the same mother; he didn't know his grandparents, in the photograph of them that sits on the chest of drawers in Léon and Hélène's bedroom they are already old and holding themselves stiffly in their oversized clothes, his grandmother has the hint of a moustache; they're sad because they've lost two sons in the war, the First World War, Léon has explained it to him. Gabrielle doesn't look like anybody, she is his mother, she lives in Paris, she comes twice a year, one week at Christmas and three weeks in August. When she's not here, people call her Gaby when they talk about her, the shutters and window of her bedroom are opened, to air it, and people think about her because, in this house, there is time and space to think about others who are far away. He prefers it when Gabrielle is a long way away, but he says nothing. He kissed her at the station, he smelled her perfume from Paris, it's the scent of arrivals and departures, and he can still smell it in his nose and throat, he is still breathing it in, he chews on it, swallows it and gulps it down. In the summer, at Figeac, his mother does not use perfume; she washes a lot, takes her time, she says that the heat ruins perfume. André listens to his mother and doesn't ask any questions, ever. Gabrielle wears light-coloured dresses, tailored to suit her narrow waist, that barely expose her calves, her ankles, her wrists, her neck. She hides away from the sun, doesn't swim, not anymore. She has just turned forty-seven, he has done the sums and worked out that it is old to be a mother, even if she still looks tall and bright in her Parisian dresses. When the locomotive's hot, square muzzle appeared at the end of the platform, Léon leaped into the carriage to find a good spot to stash the Parisienne's suitcases. That's how Léon talks, he has his own words that André just loves; they're words that set things right, that make people laugh, or smile, that provide comfort. He would rather Hélène and Léon were his real parents, and his cousins his real sisters. He would rather that, but he has always known the truth. Gabrielle is his mother and nobody knows his father. He has one, but nobody knows him. His father could certainly be living in Paris, but not with his mother; or he could live in Lyon, or in Marseille, in a big city far away. He could not live in a small place like Figeac without everybody knowing he was André's father. No unknown fathers in Figeac. For some days now, without knowing why, André has been wondering if this father would have wanted to know him, André, if he would like to know him. He has an unknown father, and that means he too is an unknown son. He hesitates, he's thinking hard, the words slide around. They are heading home from the station on foot, it's not far at all, he's trailing along behind his cousins, Hélène and Léon are a long way ahead. *Pépé* and *mémé* never come to the station; Gabrielle goes to their place to say goodbye to them and they always tell her the same thing, to be careful up there, in Paris. André doesn't know what his mother, who seems to be so solid, so swift, so efficient, is supposed to be careful about. Children have to be careful, old people too, when they become frail and slow, but grown-ups have nothing to fear, especially not his mother. He tries to work it out, his cousins are walking ahead of him and he hears their mingling voices. He feels the bite of the mid-afternoon heat on the nape of his neck his back his bare calves. He would like not to ruminate, not to ruminate anymore; another one of Léon's words for the thoughts that don't leave you alone, which dig a hole in your belly and press down on your chest. He ruminates and, for the first time, wonders if this unknown father is aware that he, ten-year-old André Léoty, exists. He stops in his tracks, just short of the entrance gate to the courtyard, under the plane tree. The question grips him; he senses, in his legs his arms his belly, that it's too big for him. He struggles, he thinks about the grammar they are being taught by their school master. He likes school his teacher the grammar, and the other subjects, he is not troubled by any of it. He would have liked also to go to Sunday school with the other children his age; but his mother would rather he didn't, she had said, he is baptised and that is enough; Hélène and Léon did not insist and he thinks he understands that the lady who teaches Sunday school and the priest, whom he knows, like everybody in Figeac, must not be altogether comfortable with the sons of unknown fathers. Unknown is a qualifying adjective, he's certain of it, he can count on that, on grammar. An unknown son for an unknown father. He would share with this father an adjective with two syllables, the first of which is a negative prefix and the second a past participle. Standing at the gate, in the full sun, seared by the sun, he is sure of his grammar. So, one adjective in common; but he, André, ten years old, has an advantage over this father. He, André, ten years old, knows that this father exists, obviously, or existed before his birth, whereas this father perhaps does not know that he has this son, a son, André Léoty, ten years old, Léoty is his mother's surname, and Hélène's maiden name; he likes those words, maiden name, his mother must have been a young woman with a maiden name too, he guesses that women are maidens before they have children, but women who are old unmarried mothers, like his mother, do not simply remain maidens for longer than the others; people talk about maidens and children of old parents; his cousins are maidens and he is the child of old parents; he cannot imagine his mother ever having been a maiden, not like his cousins are; Hélène yes, but not his mother. He would have to ask Hélène, but he doesn't ask, he doesn't dare.

André Léoty, ten years old, standing in the sun at the gate to Hélène and Léon's house, on 17 August 1934, a little before four o'clock in the afternoon, is the unknown son of that unknown father. This son is returning from the station in Figeac where the train bound for Paris is carrying away his mother, Gabrielle. His mother, that father, this son; he also knows the difference between the possessive adjective, for his mother, and the demonstrative adjectives, for that father and this son. Léon would say the difference is as plain as day, that they're each singing a different tune. At school, the teacher has them recite lists, all the grammar lists, and André never makes a mistake, especially in front of his school master whom he will have again for the whole of his fifth year of primary school. The teacher, the school, the lists, unknown, this father, unknown son, André takes a deep breath, like Hélène says you have to do when the moles start gnawing at your soul. Hélène has her own sayings too and he remembers them all because they rhyme. It's a game they play, he and Hélène, the rhyming game. She knows La Fontaine's fables which she continued to learn by heart, even after she finished primary school and received her certificate. Hélène has her certificate, Léon doesn't. Gabrielle is a nurse, she was a nurse for a long time, in Aurillac, in the Cantal, where they never go, but not in Paris; André does not really understand what it is his mother does in Paris. They hear her talk about the office, the warehouse, the shop. He does not see her caring for people, Hélène yes, but not Gabrielle. Thoughts of Gabrielle, of her sharp perfume, of the train, the platform, swim behind his eyes. He leans on the gate, with his shoulders his back his thighs; he settles in against the warm gate, under the plane tree that embraces him in its gentle shade. He thinks about lists, about his teacher; the moles calm down. No moles in the fables of La Fontaine that he recites with Hélène, in unison or in parts, following her lead. Léon loves it when they do that, he asks for it again and again. The cousins tease; they're eighteen, seventeen and fifteen years old, they're tall, they laugh, they are his *cousines-sœurs*, his sister-cousins, his *cousines-fleurs*, his flower cousins. He thinks about their twirling whirling, their delight. He wonders if they know about the moles, if they have them inside their chest, too, or lower down, in their belly, beneath their navel. Perhaps the moles don't dare gnaw at the chests of girls, of cousins, of sisters. Girls' chests. He inhales the warm air again, a small gulp. His mother has left, left again, back to her Paris, for almost five months. When she returns, he will have grown even stronger, he will have finished almost five months of school with Monsieur Brunet who is going to prepare him for the entrance exam into sixth grade. The plane tree rustles almost imperceptibly in the white heat of the afternoon, as if sighing. André senses danger beyond the plane tree and elsewhere, he is in a hurry to grow stronger, but he likes that sigh of the plane tree. Hélène is the only person he can talk to about the plane tree's sigh, he can't talk to his cousins who would poke fun and who have already started calling him Martine. Because of Lamartine, a poet they like. He doesn't like him; he'll take La Fontaine any day of the week. The plane tree sighs. His mother is further and further away. Sigh rhymes with smile, and chest with breast. He thinks about his cousins' chests; he can feel them against him when they hug him tight. His cousins hug him often, they've always done that. They're terrible when they tease him but he loves more than anything the nest of their arms, and the round warmth of their breasts under fabric. He says the word breast only to himself, in the secrecy of his own mouth. He knows he is very lucky to have his cousins; he understands that other boys, often, don't have any chests, or breasts. They look at them, they think about them, they talk about them among themselves. He has already heard the big boys who are taking their certificate talking in the covered yard, he has a feeling that it's rare and difficult for them to touch a girl's chest through any fabric. It's not that they're hoping to see them, the breasts, the chests, not truly. He doesn't get to see them either, his cousins don't show them to him, but they hug him tight, and he feels them, and it's heavenly. The plane tree rustles, it is no longer sighing. A hint of wind, a light thread, quivers in the hot, blue air. André breathes. He looks at his hands. Your pianist's hands, his mother says; she talks about André's hands a lot, about his wrists, about the piano lessons he should take. He thinks his wrists are too narrow and his hands too long. He could almost feel embarrassed by those fingers which seem to go on forever. Fortunately his feet are normal. Hélène says it's the same for pups too, who have big paws and a little body; it will all sort itself out in the end. When he finishes growing, his too-long hands will be back in proportion with the rest of his body. That's what Hélène and Claire, his favourite cousin, the middle one, tell him, and he believes them. He's waiting. He knows you have to wait, children wait. He doesn't want to take piano lessons. Fortunately you can't take lessons in Figeac, you'd have to worry about going all the way perhaps to Cahors for lessons. Gabrielle tosses words out into the air, but she does not insist, and then she leaves again, with her harsh perfume, her Parisian dresses, and her piano. He hears his name bouncing about on the breeze, it's Claire, she has been calling him, several times; she says, are you coming Dadou we're off for a swim at Le Jaladis, come on. Happiness leaps through his bones, he leaves the gate, the plane tree, Gabrielle's piano, the train and the station. He is ten years old and the summer is endless. Claire is calling him. The three girls will flash past on their bicycles, and Hélène too. Claire will carry him on her luggage rack, she always goes ahead of the others, they glide into the light and are swallowed up. André doesn't weigh a thing, that's what Claire says, Dadou is like a bird, you can't feel him behind you. He holds onto Claire by the waist, he's going with her, Claire's waist is warm and slight. Claire doesn't lean forward, she holds herself upright. The line of her shoulders, the red cascade of her sugar-strewn hair, the blond straw hat, one of her father's old hats that she has revived with a bright blue ribbon, they are André's entire horizon; and once again the world is perfect. At Le Jaladis, the green water is luminous under the tufted arcs of willow. The banks are steep, you can twist your ankles on the sharp stones, Hélène has a long swim, he loves the stripey swimsuit that Claire has picked out for him and the pale bodies of his cousins are a vivid bouquet in the dancing light.

Wednesday, 20 June 1923

PAUL'S HANDS ARE a thing of wonder. Gabrielle never tires of Paul's long hands. She has known since the outset that he will leave, that he will leave her, because she is sixteen years older than he is and she has taught him all there is to know about women, something for which a man like him could never forgive any woman. Paul is a pup, young wild cunning; he pays court, he forages for nectar, he oozes velvety glances, he hones himself, sharpens himself, he has learned quickly; he sinks in his fangs, he will be capable of anything, he will be disreputable. He is her type of man, she has known it a long time; she will be torn apart, as never before, it is the price she must pay, the cost of intoxication. She has never been keen on the gentle types, nor the kind ones; she needs the firm hand, the confident manner; she is drawn to the blazing, the blustering, the bedazzling, to the passionate ones who sear everything they touch. She had known what was happening from the first glance, in the infirmary of the boys' lycée in Aurillac, despite the regulation blue pyjamas and the bronchitis, except that this time, circumstances were lending her a slim advantage; the boy showed promise and she had a little more than two years to bring him to hand. She had made enquiries, with the utmost discretion, as to Paul's pedigree. The family ran a hotel, which also served as a restaurant and café, in a large village, at the other end of the département, on the edge of the Puy-de-Dôme. The father had been elected and re-elected for years to both the local council and the canton and was furiously ambitious. The third generation male offspring of these rural clans were expected to leave for Paris to pursue their law, or medicine. Paul would follow suit and abide by paternal injunctions. He fully intended to carve out for himself a place in the bright lights of the capital where he would fly the flag of the family name. The old world back home would be too small for him, too slow, too worn; the war's long bloodletting had planed back the villages, leaving families resigned and drained, preserved in an apparently endless period of mourning. Paul Lachalme would like to live, to shine, to have it all and partake of the ripe fruit; he would not end up as some provincial notary, paternal and paunchy, with copious children. He used to say as much; in Aurillac, already, he would summon up the future in Gabrielle's blue room, get carried away and turn circles, like a fox cub in a cage, between bed and mirrored wardrobe, in the well-heated bedroom on the top floor of 18 rue des Carmes; he had the Paris bar in his sights, the oratorical flights of barristerial robes, the memorable pleadings and the glory of redemptive or damning words. He would leave medicine to his brother who had the compassionate touch. Mademoiselle Léoty's apartment was snug and the building had two entrances, one of which, discreetly, permitted indulgence of many an impulse. She lived in a closeted part of town where everybody was watchful and made it their business to know everything about everyone, especially about that nurse who was protective enough of her freedom to live alone, a long way from her family, and to persist with home visits for her patients, before she was appointed to the sole position at the boys' lycée, a position which became available upon the retirement of the ancient and unappealing incumbent. Several men, invariably enough married, had availed themselves of the surreptitious entrance to rue des Carmes and Gabrielle's blue bedroom. Paul Lachalme was the youngest, the most intoxicating and the most dangerous. In Paris, Gabrielle's bedroom walls were also decorated in blue stretched fabric. Paul's appearances there were becoming more and more infrequent; he had other irons in the fire, Gabrielle felt it, knew it. Nothing was said, it went beyond words and she would not fight it. Paul was slipping between her fingers and would soon erase himself from her life. He had grand tastes, could aspire to a fine marriage, but also and especially to the effective network of people that carefully selected mistresses know how to curate, keen to procure a thousand useful favours for the brand new lover, through the intervention of well-heeled and well-connected husbands. Gabrielle had a nose for and guessed at this manoeuvring more than she knew of it for certain. She was not at all familiar with the social circles and milieux frequented by Paul and had not even tried to seek acceptance into them herself. She did not aspire to anything; she had followed him to Paris, had arrived there in his wake but not with him. He had always known how to keep his distance; no lovers' outings, no attending a performance together, no happy student gatherings around the table. No Sunday roasts for her, as her mother would have said, had she been able to conjure up the slightest notion of the unusual life this firstborn daughter, whose resolute desire for independence she had always found terrifying, would one day lead in Paris. Gabrielle tosses her head on the pillow, blinks. As long as Paul is there, stretched out next to her, on the bed, in the blue room, as long as he is smoking silently, as long as they are naked together, she has no wish to think about the years in Aurillac, about the headiness of their beginnings, about that acerbic and long-dead mother, nor the limpid conjugality of Hélène, her perfect next-born sister.

She blinks and swallows the moment, drinks it inhales it, and draws nourishment from it, through to her bones. She stops herself tasting, again and again, with molten mouth, the gentle crease of Paul's almond eyes and the perfect hollow of his ears; tenderness is a luxury, a risk; he would

be riled; he changes and withdraws. He is ever more handsome, his star will burn long and bright, and he approaches
her, overcome with self-admiration. Gabrielle listens to him
and plays her part opposite him to perfection. He likes that
about her; he says, your ear and your velvet. The velvet is
her skin, and it was she who had prompted him with the
word. He excels at appropriating the words of others, he
adopts them and makes them his own, to the point where
very soon he has forgotten their origins. She listens to him;
his voice is no longer the same, the sharp edges of any accent
have been dulled, it has assumed a curious timbre, at once
metallic and resonant, slightly nasal; Gabrielle sinks into
that voice, loses herself in the meanderings of its inflections.
Paul's left hand lingers on her hip, slides towards the hollow
of her groin, the top of her thigh. Paul is insatiable, he is
not miserly with his body and its juices, not yet. He makes
an effort, he provides, one could say almost gallant and
generous. She ought to perhaps also teach him how to wait,
and make himself desirable, how to push up the bidding.
He would certainly have a talent for it. He gives himself a
shake, charmingly. He always gives himself a shake afterwards. It is a remnant from childhood, a cry from within,
something that has survived from that glorious little boy he
must have been, in those early years, between his parents'
hotel and the village school where the mayor's two sons were
viewed as pampered princes, the stuff of miracles. There
had been another child, another son who had been his twin,

and what Paul would recount of the prolonged death of his brother, whose name he never uttered, was, in Gabrielle's mind, his burning secret, the pain at his epicentre, his open wound. Paul smoked his second cigarette; he would always smoke two, he had his own lover's routines. Gabrielle had no desire to think about this martyred twin, Paul used that word; Paul's first memories, at four and a half, four years, eight months and twenty-four days to be quite precise, he would clarify, were memories of a drawn-out cataclysm that had started when he was woken by a scream on the morning of Thursday, 25 April 1908 and that had furrowed the family ever since, as one would plough a field. That was Paul's image and Gabrielle did not like it; she considered it false, affected and attention-seeking, she did not like the word martyred either, which he uttered with a sort of anguished voluptuousness, but she had never said that to him. She understood that this particular emphasis was all he had found to create a bulwark between himself and those frenzied hours. Paul would recount how Armand's death had driven his mother and his aunt to religion, his brother Georges to perfection, despite his mere three and a half years, his father to ambition, and himself to an untamed ferocity. Gabrielle would readily have blended those last two descriptions but again remained silent. She had fewer and fewer opportunities to comment; Paul's childhood was receding, ebbing away; rarer were the occasions when he would tell stories, he was becoming more succinct, gagging the young boy just as he was embarking on his adult life. The June evening was endless and the light danced through the plane trees in the oval-shaped public garden of the cité de Trévise. When she had arrived in Paris, Gabrielle had not been surprised to find in the hidden corners of the ninth arrondissement the haughty, rustling trees that had framed the gateway of her sister's house in Figeac. She had never had a taste for the countryside; she was bored by the bucolic; too much greenery, that was her customary verdict. She liked her scenery to be civilised, tamed, controlled and would pay only absent-minded attention to the landscape when, twice a year, she would cross France by train on her way back to the Lot and to her three nieces, who were more glorious with every visit, to Hélène, majestic in her unassuming happiness, and to placid Léon, purring away and indefatigable. Gabrielle wondered how, for more than thirty-three years, she could have lived anywhere else except Paris, and was eternally grateful to Paul for forcing her to that reluctant decision. She had extracted herself, had left Aurillac, Figeac, the Cantal and the Lot, the suspicious looks and knowing silences. When he had discovered that she would follow him to Paris, Paul had displayed neither enthusiasm, nor annoyance; he had been flattered, even if he had said nothing of it, but she had understood that she would have to know her place. Three years later, she continued to be dazzled by the hard-won freedom she enjoyed every day. She did not explore every possibility, did not test its limits; when it came down to it, she had continued the clandestine habits of the boarding school with Paul; she could not, at more than thirty-five years of age, expect a pear tree to produce apples; the lawful and official loves of Paul Lachalme would play out elsewhere, with other women. She had neither the requisite age, body, nor background to venture out onto those brutal hunting grounds. That chapter had been closed without really ever having been opened. For six weeks, almost seven now, she had counted in silence while Paul took his time in the little bathroom, in the mirror she could see the perfect line of his shoulders, the smooth, fair nape of his neck, his back, his hips; for six weeks and four days, then, she had been in a state of utter isolation. She knew her body, she understood what was happening to her; she was not some naïve young girl, she had a few flying hours under her belt, her brother-in-law had said, in his jovial, provincial manner. She found herself at once discombobulated and curiously calm. She no longer knew quite what to think. Why dwell on Léon's words; how had she allowed herself to be caught out; she was a nurse, she was thirty-six years old, almost thirty-seven, she had never been pregnant, why now; and to this man, she hesitated over the word, man young man lover lad rascal, she was hesitating over the word but facing the facts; of all the males she had encountered in her life, Paul Lachalme was the one least capable of being a father; and not just because he was only twenty-one years old. He would always be too full of himself, it would never change, she could expect nothing else. A trick played by this soon-forty-year-old woman's body of hers, that is what she was up against, what she was being forced to confront, without panicking or torturing herself too much; all she knew was that she would not do the rounds of the backyard abortionists and she would keep the child; it would be raised in the Lot, Hélène would take care of it. Standing in the evening light, Gabrielle surveyed the contour of her breasts, their firm white fullness dazzling in the bevelled mirror of the tall wardrobe; breasts that were invigoratingly full, glorious, sole witnesses as yet to her new condition. Paul, however, had still not noticed a thing. Paul no longer saw her.

Tuesday, 5 March 1935

PAUL DOES NOT KNOW if he is sad. He is moved by his mother, and he is fooling everybody, his brother, his aunt, as he sheds tears for his mother, for that which has struck her down and plunged her into the irretrievable state of widow and old woman. She has just turned fifty-two, on 6 February. His mother's is the only birthday he knows. He respected his father but, in his younger years, had feared him for too long ever to feel perfectly at ease in his company. The childhood habit had remained, leaving Maître Paul Lachalme, barrister-at-law at the Paris bar, starched and stiff, as though on high alert with a father who had always, when it came to Paul, vacillated between pride and exasperation. At stake was his mother, condemned to be caught between father and son, and doing her best to reconcile the irreconcilable. Georges did not participate in the charade and did not partake of that stale bread; Georges did not remember those dreadful hours and had not had to outlive a dead twin. Pale and aloof in their neck ties, flanking their mother in full mourning, and escorted by their no less grief-stricken aunt, Paul and Georges Lachalme stood before the prideful vault in the blue and biting cold of the high country. They shook hands, kissed cheeks, stammered the customary formulae, recognised faces that had aged, held back smiles and masked the bewilderment to which they would later confess during the sharing of brotherly confidences in the privacy of the warm, subdued house. The first house comes from his mother's side of the family; it was added to by his father, and sits next to a vast building in which the hotel-restaurant is comfortably prospering, but the hollow nest, the warm cradle of his beginnings, is to be found in his mother's rooms, where she was born and grew up with his aunt, three years her junior, in the meandering succession of connecting rooms filled with gleaming furniture that is the smug kingdom of the Santoire sisters, Lucie and Marguerite. Despite his father and his grand airs, despite his rages, whims and other passing fancies, Marguerite never ceded her ground. She held firm, silent and stern, perhaps resigned, without ever daring to voice one word louder than another in front of that cutting brother-in-law who tolerated her by virtue only of the domestic chores she graciously proffered to the household. Paul tells himself that they will finally be at peace, the two sisters; he thinks of them as the sisterhood, but he senses that this Parisian description is not fitting in this place and at this time, here in Chanterelle, under a thousand stars, on 5 March 1935, on the evening of his all-powerful father's funeral. Even if his word rings false for the two sisters, the matter will indeed be settled; he knows his father's affairs have been smoothly handled and are very lucrative, the bulk of the money secured in land and in bricks and mortar. Lucie and Marguerite will have something to fall back on and will be able to enjoy a quiet life without having to struggle on their own to run the hotel-restaurant; he will not waste any time before bringing somebody in to manage it on the best possible terms. He has his contacts, he knows the right people. He will stay on for a few days, at least until the end of the week, long enough to agree matters with "the sisters", who never stand in his way. He smiles at his use of this casual anglicism and stretches out between the white sheets that bear his embroidered monogram. Paul Lachalme is at the height of his physical prowess, the Chanterelle winter is stirring the blood, he is going to take charge of the family property, ensure the comfort of his mother and aunt, and graciously attend to his own interests, as only he knows how, in his capacity as a dutiful son of the family. His brother, Georges, is the good father of the family, and he trusts Paul unswervingly. Georges is securing, has already secured, the family line, and will preserve the family name. A second birth is imminent in Orléans, where Georges has settled thanks to a most advantageous marriage. Paul would happily be wary of his sister-in-law, also a doctor, and an only child with an impressive Orléans lineage, a woman confident of her prerogatives and very ill-disposed to being appraised or led down the garden path by her brother-in-law, even if he was the firstborn son of the siblings and had been elevated forever more by his mother, aunt and brother to the rank of living god. Madeleine has stayed in Orléans, the child is expected within the fortnight, they are hoping for a boy. Paul grimaces at the painful memory of Georges, overcome with joyful tenderness, settling into Paul's arms his niece and goddaughter, Pauline, a hearty three-month-old infant, pink and heavy, and bundled up in white. Honour to whom honour is due; he would be the godfather of the firstborn child, but also and more importantly of the first male. He had extracted that promise from Georges upon Pauline's birth, under the suspicious eye of Madeleine who could not offer up the services of any godfather, every able-bodied man in the family, her brother and three cousins, having fallen at Les Éparges, Verdun and in the Dardanelles. Fallen; Madeleine says fallen; she does not say killed in action nor ever lapse into the religious platitudes that are the customary source of feminine consolation. Madeleine is magnificent. She is quite something, a lioness, a queen, a woman who will not allow successive pregnancies to be her undoing. Paul has an eye, he knows how to judge, how to gauge, he is rarely mistaken; there is no doubt Madeleine is made of fine materials, the highest grade. With assets to boot: houses and apartment buildings in Orléans, properties in Beauce, some hunting grounds in Sologne. A career in medicine, which she expects to resume immediately after the birth, tops it off; a woman of such an ilk is not for marrying. There is no handicap for Georges, this filly will take out every race by several lengths, and Paul does not like that. His brother is utterly besotted by his imperious Madeleine, but he would have been better off marrying an appropriately innocent girl with nothing much between the ears and who came well-endowed; life would have been simpler – for everybody.

In the dining room, the Condat carillon is the first to strike twelve with its bold chimes; Paul waits for it to run its course, thought momentarily suspended. Before heading to bed, he has wound up all six of the clocks in the house again, including the chiming ones. It is a job for a man, an eldest son. The Condat carillon booms out; thus has the clock ever been known after it was inherited from a maternal great-uncle, a notary from that largish village, the administrative seat of the canton that sits wedged at the confluence of the rivers Rhue, Bonjon and Santoire. Paul is fond of his rivers, he knows them spiritually, physically, especially the Santoire, which bears his mother's family name, unless it is the other way around, a proper trout-fishing river, wilful wily meaty lively. A shiver runs through him under the heavy, cool sheets; fishing, hunting, he has always been madly passionate about them both, a passion akin to his appetite for women. In fact, he felt it very early on; it is the same thing, the same game, similar chase, similar intoxication. The clock sends out its second salvo, at once hoarse and crystalline. Paul pictures his father again, quick and precise, demonstrating to him and to Georges how it was done, with the dogs, with the game, furred and feathered both, and also with the gleaming creatures to be found in the water. In that regard, and that regard only, Georges, more patient and no less determined, could have outdone his elder brother, but the habit of precedence had been set and Paul knew of no better hunting or fishing companion than his brother. Since his marriage to the sumptuous Madeleine, the two brothers had been granted access to the family property, in Sologne. They relished their time there, a few hours from Paris; it was a world away from the high country where the luxurious sophistication of such hunting pursuits remained unknown. Alas, Madeleine too enjoyed the hunt, when she was not bridled by pregnancies; she was physically daring and an excellent shot, which had dazzled his father, who remained otherwise dumbfounded in the face of such feminine bounty. Paul turns over in the warm bed; he is not sure what exactly his mother and aunt make of Madeleine. Georges chose her, she is the mother of his children and that is all there is to it. The Santoire sisters know how to behave, they will maintain their even temper, and will cherish above all else the marvellous children who are the future of the family household. The large upstairs bedroom has already been refurbished, refreshed and reconfigured to receive the infants in August. His father had offered no objections, leaving the women to it in that old part of the house; in any event he had demonstrated very little enthusiasm when it came to Pauline, the first born; he was waiting for the male offspring, whom now he would not know. He had been about to turn seventy. Nobody had known he had a weak heart and nobody had ever suffered from that condition in a family where unyielding elderly were commonplace. Paul remembered his grandfather's three brothers, desiccated, nimble old fellows who, at more than eighty years of age, would still go hunting in the woods around Savignat and up on the Manicaudies plateau, where they had all continued to live, hunkered down on tiny hidden-away farms that were cherished as if they were perfect principalities. This established tradition of bachelorhood justified in part his own status as a free agent, which nonetheless used to vex his mother. She would let it be known through the repeated voicing of her concern about his masculine household, about what he was eating, and who was doing his laundry and housework; a bachelor was not well cared for, nor pampered; obviously he would be indulging in all manner of excessive behaviour harmful to his health. Paul Lachalme smiles beneath the paunch of the eiderdown and quilted covers. His mother cannot imagine his life and can hardly conceive of his passion for women. Out of respect, he moderates his ardour for the three weeks of his summer sojourns, limiting himself, for health reasons also, to clandestine renewals of contact with a former acquaintance, who is accommodating and light-hearted, albeit a little worn at the edges, and who lives in

Nice but spends the month of August at a family property in Le Vaysset near Condat. It's a pretty part of the world, Le Vaysset, but a dreadful name, short, perfunctory and ugly on the ear; Santoire was something else altogether, it had a very particular feel, gave you a sense of the rivers and of the people. Chanterelle, Santoire, the childhood bedroom where, in the year he turned twenty, his narrow teenager's bed had been replaced with the vain optimism of a marital bed, and the woods, and the meadows, and the hunts which set off in the pearlescent dawns, and the long hours devoted to tenacious fishing expeditions, and the merest bend in the steep road which snaked between hedges in the cathedralesque light, all of it stuck to his ribs, with no trace of nostalgia, with the brutal joy of belonging. He belonged and all of that belonged to him. This gift he had always had of feeling at home, of feeling legitimate and desirable, wherever he was, it came from here, from Chanterelle, from that name, from his mother, from the house, the land, the raw air. When in Venice, at the Royal Danieli no less, where he had briefly stayed the previous autumn with a very beautiful woman, still some way out of his league, he had thought back to his bedroom in Chanterelle, to the sheets, embroidered laundered pressed, readied by his mother and by his aunt. He had thought himself back there in his skin, it was his secret and so it would remain. People knew he was from the Cantal in the Auvergne, from a farming family; but more they would not know. Mystery enhanced the lustre; it was a formula by which he stuck and one he often bore in mind when it came to women he had conquered, had hollowed out, who had grown stale. He was not going to get any sleep. In a few hours, he would get up; he would find Georges in the kitchen, with a bowl of strong coffee and the generous pieces of bread their mother could not resist spreading with butter. They would remain there, all three of them, around the table, and his father's place would be empty. Georges had business in Orléans, he would say that life must prevail over death, he would head off under the sharp stars into the night, furnished with warm brioches and a beautifully woven white blanket for the imminent infant. At the cemetery, after the procession of well-wishers, Georges had whispered to him that if it were a boy, he would be called Armand. Madeleine, whose eldest brother of the same name had been killed at Les Éparges, had agreed. Madeleine this, Madeleine that, enough about Madeleine. Georges was not afraid of that first name and perhaps he was right; how could he have any memory of Armand? Paul had no desire to remember, but he did, the memory would resurface, it would overwhelm him; the evening prayer in the big bedroom upstairs, their two cots on either side of the blue rug on which their mother would kneel to say the Our Father and Hail Mary, Armand on the left, he on the right, the murmuring of the jumble of prayers like the song of a green river over a bed of pebbles. Other things float to the surface, things he would like to forget when he sleeps, a scream hurled into the morning, the flayed-animal growls of the brother who took so long to die, and the wild eyes of the culpable maid.

Wednesday, 20 January 1960

HÉLÈNE IS KNITTING for Antoine. Booties and bonnets, the family knows that is her department and expects as much of her. She has always had a feeling that Juliette and André's child would be a boy. They call them Hélène's intuitions and they carry the weight of the oracle. She and Léon have already seven granddaughters who are growing up in Saint-Céré, Cahors and Bergerac. They see them often, they come, they go, they stay, they go again, in lively clusters of two and three and four; Léon, who prides himself on his knowledge of bullfighting, calls them a *manade* of cousins, after the herds of Camargue cattle. Hélène switches off the radio, she is alone, Léon is in Cahors, putting up shelves for Claire, whose husband has butter fingers and could not hammer in a nail without doing himself an injury; Claire's eldest daughter devours books, day and night, she has only just turned sixteen and has a good head on her shoulders, she has skipped ahead a year at school and wants to understand everything, learn everything; there is talk of sending her to a prestigious lycée in Paris with very competitive entrance exams. Her parents are proud, her grandparents too, but Hélène considers her granddaughter on the young side to be leaving for boarding school in Paris where she would forget to eat and to sleep so she could keep reading and studying.

Hélène likes to knit as it keeps her hands busy and allows her mind to roam. The silence in the house envelops her; rarely is she alone and these moments are precious. Léon talks a lot, he makes noise, he turns the volume up on the radio because he is growing hard of hearing. She does not think about a life without Léon and the children, her whole horizon is filled by her family, but she knows that it is possible to live differently. Gabrielle has lived differently, still does, and the sky has not fallen on her head. The clickety-clack of her needles provides an answering rhythm to the clock's ticking. It is a blue January day; the winter light is perfect for handicrafts. She hears the voice of her mother-in-law who took the time to teach her sewing, knitting, crocheting and different embroidery stitches. Her mother could not have shown her, would have had neither the time nor the inclination. Her parents had never grown used to Gabrielle's ways; they brooded over it, they muttered in the corners, but never did they dare, not even their mother who was not, it must be said, lacking in spirit herself, confront that great horse. Hélène remembers how they would talk about her, and call her that great horse; they were bewildered, discouraged, humiliated, and angry too, a suppressed anger, the sort that lasts and eats away at you. That edge to Gabrielle, her restive filly ways which she had exhibited since childhood, left them speechless. They had perhaps been proud that she wanted to learn a profession and become a nurse. They suspected that marriage, children, an orderly and predictable life in Figeac or Saint-Céré would not be for her; but to go from that to accepting and putting up with her make-up, her outfits, her relaxed ways with men, that was a different chasm to cross. They had resigned themselves, put up with the noises, the gossip-mongering, the sidelong glances. Aurillac was not that far away, and Gabrielle was the subject of a certain degree of low-level chatter. Hélène remembered the chastened expressions and interrupted conversations when she appeared. People were keen to spare her, to protect her from any contamination, as if the disagreeable habits of her older sister may have been contagious. Hélène smiles, it is all a long time ago, her needles click, she squints and wrinkles her nose, she must finish off the bootie and she concentrates for a moment to make sure it is perfect. André and Juliette are her children, and Antoine, who has taken ten years to arrive, is her first grandson and will remain an only child. There were expectations, disappointments, complications, but it did not take a tragic turn because Juliette and André have a knack for happiness, for joy, for bright, sweet things that make one feel good. They have a flair for it and to Hélène's mind, that is as good as any victory. She, Léon, and their three girls have known how to ward off bad luck; she reels off the sayings, bad luck, victory, that seem appropriate. André got off to an unfortunate start, no father, an accident; that was the first, and only, word Gabrielle had used to describe her circumstances when she had stepped off the train in Figeac in August 1923, more than three months pregnant and apparently very comfortable with that. The customary three weeks had slipped past, day after day, in a silence that was less and less embarrassed; no more questions were asked after Gabrielle had announced, on the first evening, sitting with them and the girls at the table in the kitchen that opened out onto the orchard, I'm keeping this child, he will not know his father, he will bear my name, Léoty is a fine name, he will be born in Paris, and I'm asking that you, Hélène, Léon, and you girls, all of you, bring him into your home and raise him until I am able to look after him myself in the best possible circumstances, if you agree, he will be the son and little brother you never had, and each month I shall send provision for his food and board. Her grey eyes were unblinking, her voice had not softened, the matter of her forthcoming child was apparently settled. It was only to her and Léon, that same evening, once the girls were in bed, that Gabrielle had again brandished the son card; she had repeated, in the warm night air of the garden, it's an accident, but it will give you a son, and a brother for my nieces. They had allowed two days to go past before speaking of it again, on a stormy evening enveloped by the rich scent of a summer downpour, a smell that surfaces in Hélène's memory and catches her by surprise, thirty-seven years later, her two hands rounded into a shell around the pair of booties on her knees, pale yellow, fresh butter, she thinks, fresh butter. Her memory works by smells, Gabrielle's Parisian perfumes, the sleepy breath of each of the three girls, and then André's, when leaning over them, in the evening, in the quiet of the bedroom, before heading to bed herself, the first strawberries of the season at Tuesday's market, Léon's shaving cream. Her repertoire is never-ending, she reels it off sometimes, as if to gather together her life, between two fables of La Fontaine, in whom little by little she has lost interest because it is much less fun to recite them alone than with André. In August 1923, the storm had broken in the heavy evening after a scorching day, the girls had been wide-eyed; Léon had remained quiet, Hélène guessing at his unfathomable astonishment. Questions had poured forth, will he have his own room, what will he be called, will it be a long time that he stays with us, will he go to school here, will he know who his mother is. She had held back the flood, with Gabrielle, before then remaining speechless when Claire had asked Gabrielle how she knew it would be a boy.

Hélène had gone up to Paris for the birth, had remained close by her sister and assisted the midwife, an acquaintance of Gabrielle, whose vigorous mannerisms and flowery language inspired perfect confidence. Gabrielle appeared to be made to bring children into the world; she had given birth without any of the usual complications, despite her thirty-seven years and, observing the creature with a dubious eye, had declared André to be the chosen name, demonstrating without a pause all the necessary skills for handling an infant whom she would allow to depart for the Lot, in the arms of his aunt, less than three weeks after his birth, with no discernible hesitation. In Figeac, everything was ready; upstairs where the girls' bedrooms were, Léon had emptied out a small room which until then had generally been used for storing overflow from the house. The parquetry floor had been scraped back and scrubbed, the walls repainted white, the family cradle had been refurbished and a cot hauled out of the attic along with the high chair and a light chest of drawers. Crocheted curtains, bedding, little outfits, there was no shortage of useful items in the house. Hélène and *mémé* had washed and freshened things up, ironed an entire trousseau. They were expecting a living baby doll, it would be a serious matter, the real thing; there would be no dropping him, perhaps he would cry in the night, they would take it in turns to give him the bottle. Hélène kneaded Antoine's yellow booties absentmindedly and felt a violent emotion flood over her, which shook her through and through, as had happened in February of 1924, on the 8th to be precise, a Friday, at the exact moment when she had stepped down onto the station platform in Figeac. Léon had put up no opposition, not for a second, André's arrival had been a triumph, an inexhaustible source of delight. Very soon, with the exception of *pépé* who remained pensive in the face of this incongruous business cooked up in Paris, everybody would be wondering, without admitting as much to themselves, how they had managed to live until then without André, his first smiles, his boundless appetite, his babbling, his chortling, his enthusiasm, his sweet-natured energy and his gentle spirit. His presence had worked upon the house like an uplifting song, despite the loose tongues and the hollow created in his life by the absence of a father. That year, Gabrielle had come down at Easter time; dashingly attired, she had dispatched a few regulation bottles, showered compliments on her three nieces for their extraordinary nappy-changing skills, which she considered a thankless task, and demonstrated to everybody her utter satisfaction at seeing this ever so amiable child, her own creation, occupy a position in the household that had so manifestly been carved out just for him. Nobody had taken offence at anything; *pépé* had grumbled in his corner, as yet unaware that he too would end up besotted by this errant grandson for whom he would, before dying, find the time to impart the skilled art of fly-fishing on the banks of the Lot. Life had continued, with André, but Hélène knew that for more than thirty years something had been eating away at the heart of that boy, that man, who was her son, and Gabrielle's. André loved Léon, but he had not used him to fill the place of a father, a place that had remained void, vacant, and vertiginous, despite Léon's presence and despite also the powerful link which the years in the maquis had created between André and Pierre, his group leader. Pierre had been killed in a motorbike accident, on 14 July 1956, and the loss had hit André hard. With tender and precise gestures, Hélène places the three pairs of booties and the two bonnets intended for Antoine into a rectangular box lined with blue tissue paper. She has stood up and walked away from the window and the hastening January dusk. The days were lengthening, however, that much was evident, even if the plane trees at the gate would remain bare against the sky for some time yet. Those trees had borne witness to her entire life; she could still see André and the girls, nestled under their perennial shade, busy, engrossed in games or mysterious children's business. She was seventy-two years old and felt herself to be strong; Léon was approaching seventy-four but was not at all showing his age. Antoine would also burble away under the plane trees, and perhaps he would take his first steps there. Juliette and André would leave him with them to mind; ten years of marriage had washed over them, they were a passionate couple, Hélène was certain of it; some signs were a giveaway, certain gestures light but confident, moving. She would not have said as much in respect of the households, incidentally not a word she would use when talking about André and Juliette, the households of her daughters, more sensible, more stale and, at least when it came to her eldest daughter, whom she sensed to be anxious and suffering, perhaps more at risk. At the end of the week, André and Juliette would be here, in the house which they would fill with their energy. Hélène closes the box, hunts around in the top drawer of the chest, the gift drawer, for a green ribbon which she ties in a careful bow. She had avoided pink and blue, had confined herself to yellows, greens and providential white, but she was calm and had good reason to be so. A boy had arrived. A generation later, Antoine would be to the *manade* of his female cousins what André had been to the girls, a living doll, an exquisite prince, a piece of fruit in which to delight.

Saturday, 21 April 1962

JULIETTE AND ANDRÉ consider boulevard Arago to be an elegant street; Juliette adds that it is pretty; that is the word she uses, repeating it to André who, having taken up position under the chestnut trees, says nothing in reply, but eyes her sceptically and asks her how a brownish burrstone wall could ever be pretty. Juliette laughs but does not let it drop; boulevard Arago is not just the Santé Prison, it is not as though that is where your father lives, although he might have various of his clients nearby, with an address like that, it's convenient, and he's an astute man, is Maître Lachalme. André relents and smiles. Indeed, number 34 is a handsome building; dressed stone, windows and balconies with wrought-iron railings and balustrades; it is obviously well-to-do, and well maintained. Maître Paul Lachalme's plate and doorknob on the double-wing door gleam in the soft, grey April evening. Juliette and André arrived in Paris the day before, a Friday, and will stay through to Monday. They had thought they would rather drive up, had dropped

Antoine in Figeac on the way through, and will pick him up on their return, and then, only then, will they perhaps tell Hélène and Léon their true reason for going to Paris, what they encountered at boulevard Arago, at number 34, what they saw, or whom they saw, if they see anybody. They walk back up the side of the boulevard with the odd numbers, all the way to place Denfert-Rochereau. The dusk is mauve, the buds on some of the chestnut trees are already appearing, and their sharp, almost preternatural green pierces the half-light. André and Juliette float in the evening and allow themselves to be cradled by the city's continuous hum, its ebb and flow, the traffic on the boulevard, the buses and cars hurtling around the square, an entire quotidian choreography, the rules of which do not appear to follow the same logic as in Toulouse, where they live a long way from the town centre. On 1 January that year, as they were surfacing, a little fuzzily, from a fun party of celebrations with friends and close family, André had said, looking Juliette directly in the eye, this year I'm going to look for him I'm going to find him I want to see him we're going up to Paris for three days at Easter you have to come with me I'm not going without you. He had drawn breath and had leaned against the fridge to down a large glass of water as he often did when they would talk in the kitchen, just the two of them. Juliette had set the coffee pot down on the table. She had waited a long time for this, ever since their wedding night, twelve years earlier. She was not annoyed with Gabrielle for having chosen that moment to let it all out and leave her, Juliette, carrying the bundle, when she was just starting her life with André, and knew what it was all about, but could perfectly well have taken fright at the gaping chasm that had opened beneath their feet. Gabrielle remained a mystery to Juliette who had the fortunate capacity not to let it trouble her. It just so happened that this peculiar and unapproachable woman had carried André in her womb; to see him with Hélène, Léon and the cousins, it was difficult to believe. This woman had provided him with his surname, Léoty, his first name, his soft brown curls, almost certainly the way he carried himself, and that was about it. There would be no further entries on the inventory. On account of the chasm. Ever since that first evening, their wedding night, they had referred to it between themselves as "the thing", or "the paternal hole", or "the Padirac Chasm"; and they did not forget it. They lived with those silences and that ghost of a father endowed with an identity, an age, a profession, an address in Paris and family property in the Cantal. This inventoried ghost led an intermittent existence in the hidden folds of their consciousness; before Antoine was born, they would rarely speak of it and it remained inconsequential. Gabrielle, with whom they would cross paths three or four times a year in Figeac, had never again ventured down the fraught path of her divulgences at their wedding. They did not ask her any questions and she did not attempt to determine whether they had already tried to identify the father's tracks and flush him out, either in Paris or from his property in the high country. When she had been informed of the impending birth, she had only commented to André: this will change things for you from the point of view of your father, you'll see. André had not pursued the matter, but he sensed, and Juliette with him, that Gabrielle was not mistaken; it would be necessary to confront the phantom, to stand before him one day, to dare, to mount the attack, to lance the old abscess which was not painful, not yet, but which would not drain of its own accord. A little more than two years had gone by, André would soon turn forty. His position as a man in the world was established, alongside Juliette and Antoine, he was fond of his job which nonetheless he had not chosen, he was becoming a man of substance, assuming responsibilities, expanding, but something, rather than somebody, was missing in the wings, was carving out more a hollow than a chasm; a chasm was too sheer, even if, as he approached forty and ever since Antoine's arrival, André felt that, far from closing up with age, as he had wanted with all his might at the age of twenty or thirty to believe it would, the fault line was going to widen and deepen; the worm was in the fruit. He had not forgotten the moles from his childhood and the iron hand that would crush his chest on certain evenings despite Hélène and the enduring air of tranquillity cultivated beneath the Figeac plane trees. So, then, they would go to Paris at Easter, to ferret out this father's tracks. They had sought confirmation in the directories which had verified the addresses and provided them with telephone numbers in Paris and in the Cantal. It would only have been a few hours' drive from Figeac to Chanterelle, they would have seen, would have known, seen and known what? Better to start with Paris; Chanterelle was too exposed, too direct; they would not pass unnoticed in Chanterelle whereas in Paris it would be easy to remain anonymous and to slip, incognito, into the wings of Paul Lachalme's life.

They would not tell Gabrielle, they would not see her; while they prepared for their paschal escapade, they realised they knew almost nothing about Gabrielle's Parisian life nor did they want to know. Hélène, who had been consulted in early January, admitted to not knowing anything about the possible state of relations between her sister and André's father. She supposed that the relationship, she also used the word affair, had been broken off even before André's birth, but she was not certain. On the first Sunday of January 1962, in the kitchen at Figeac, while Antoine had his nap, and Léon was taking his, having dozed off in his armchair in the dining room, Hélène had told them about the episode that involved André's first year of high school, a story which André had not previously heard. In 1935, André had been eleven years old and was showing undeniable promise in his school work; so Gabrielle had indicated her firm intention to take him back with her to Paris and to enrol him in a very prestigious private school, the École Alsacienne, where she was able to use her connections to get a foot in the door, Hélène remembered it all perfectly well. It had been suggested to her, she had been flattered, she was hesitating, a decision had to be made, it was a serious matter, André's future depended on it. For the first time, Hélène had seen her sister flustered, prevaricating and she had been emboldened to ask if André's father were behind this development. Given Gabrielle's reticent, evasive response, she had realised that she was probably not on the right track. So there they were then at the end of April, in 1935, and Gabrielle had appeared for three days, turning up essentially unannounced which was not at all her usual custom, only to reveal on that first evening, after the meal, just as soon as André and the girls had gone off to bed, that she was considering taking her son back to Paris, since he was so gifted, so bright, so inquisitive about everything, and focussed; she grew animated, spoke about the piano also, that lessons would be set in train up there, were it not already too late. Hélène remained silent, fixed frozen drowning in words, hands flat on her thighs, spine upright, glued to the back of her chair. Léon had leaped up, upsetting the plates in a house where nobody ever upset anything; he was clinging to the table, struggling to control the trembling of his entire body. He had said, without shouting, in a voice that was broken and rough, a voice that Hélène did not recognise, his eyes firmly holding Gabrielle's gaze, who was seated opposite him, you can't take him back, you've never had him, he is like a son to us, he is happy here, he is growing up nicely, we are making a man of him, leave him be. Hélène's voice had disappeared into these final words and Juliette had waited a moment before resting a hand gently on her shoulder. In the downstairs bedroom Antoine had woken up, his burbling could be heard through the wall, André had said, I'll take care of it, and he had left the room. Hélène had continued, I don't think that man knows he has a son. Juliette had been taken by a short rush of anger directed at Gabrielle, her secrets, her digressions, her affectations, her vague desires, her demands and her long tyranny; but anger was not Juliette's way, and there was indeed nothing to expect from Gabrielle, no recourse. They would pursue matters differently. They would bypass her. Later, in early March, they had followed the advice of Christian, who knew Paris, the city where his wife, Suzanne, had been born and where they had lived until they had married; they had booked three nights in a hotel in rue Gay-Lussac, whose name, with the exception of one letter, had seemed a good omen. *L'Hôtel des Familles, Maison Lachaume, Father & Son, established 1924*, was indeed aptly named; they had been welcomed, showered with attention by the kindly owner, a woman originally from Bretenoux but who had found herself exiled to the north of the Loire for the love of the son, Monsieur Lachaume, born in 1924, the year in which the hotel had been established, the son's name being Paul. Stunned by the coincidences, Juliette and André had been about to tell their hostess everything, and had then had a change of heart before they set off with a lighter step to find boulevard Arago early on Saturday morning. They had to carry out a reconnaissance, explore the trail, follow the scent. The discreet mention of the ground floor, below and to the left of Maître Paul Lachalme's plaque, had given them the information they needed. Without agreeing as such, they had taken a seat on a bench, fortuitously situated on the other side of the boulevard, directly opposite number 34, and they had waited for more than an hour, shoulder to shoulder, without speaking, calm and nervous, a little on edge. At about eleven o'clock, a man who looked to be André's age, or a little younger, had emerged; he had lit a cigarette with a twitchy gesture; his gaze had swept across the boulevard, taking in their bench, but not seeing them. They had started, and had both felt a similar frisson pass through them. The man had hesitated before changing his mind and disappearing back into the bowels of the building. Immediately afterwards, a woman, plump and in a hurry, had gone in, then re-emerged a few minutes later, flanked by two stocky little boys. The trio had returned twenty minutes later, the children bouncing ahead, the woman burdened with an enormous bouquet of red roses. André and Juliette had not noticed the morning disappear and were now ravenous. Christian and Suzanne had sung the praises of the nearby rue Mouffetard. It would not be said that they had allowed a whole day to go begging while waiting for the father to make an appearance. After a lunch of sausage and mashed potatoes with Cantal cheese, prepared the Aveyron way, so as to make themselves feel more at home, they would go to the Louvre. It was not as though Paris were just around the corner, and they had promised themselves not to sacrifice their entire stay to Paul Lachalme. The "Mona Lisa" could almost have been disappointing, but they were quite taken by the staggering commotion of "The Wedding at Cana" and, drunk on the colours, the figures, the motifs, they presented themselves once more, at a quarter past six, at number 34 boulevard Arago. Their step was resolute, almost military, and the surroundings felt almost familiar. First they took a photograph of André, stiff and standing squarely in front of the building. They then gave the door a push, it was simple. No sudden appearance of a concierge. At the back, on the right-hand side, a second door, heavy and gleaming, bearing the fateful name plate. André rang, for a long time, twice, three times. Something seemed to slip past behind the polished sign, a curtain along a rod perhaps, they would have sworn it, but nothing happened, nothing more. The door would not be opening. They found themselves back out on the boulevard in the mild and honeyed evening.

Sunday, 28 October 1945

GABRIELLE IS WARY of the past, she wards it off; at her age, fifty-eight, almost fifty-nine, a woman has everything to fear from her past, regrets, remorse, nostalgia, the cold iron taste of missed opportunities and the rising tide of lost illusions. Gabrielle straightens herself against the rounded back of her green armchair; she does not care at all for autumn, it's a spineless, sentimental, dreary season that she has never liked. Even if the war is over, miasmas saturate the air with a lingering stench and peace does not smell good. The first half of the forties has been interminable, and bumpy; a tunnel. Like everybody else, Gabrielle made do, as best she could. She wended her way through the grey banality of the days, Hélène sent regular and generous parcels that meant she was able to get by and, at no point, except in the June of 1940, was she tempted to retreat to Figeac for a lengthy period to allow the storm to pass while she sheltered in the family fold. She knows, she has seen it, she has understood, that her son is now a hero, a twenty-one-year-old hero. She turns the word over again and again, skirts around it, considers it and savours it. A Resistance fighter, respected, recognised, courageous, solid, reliable, loyal. She is getting used to this glorious litany, she could be proud, she probably is, but if she is proud, it is mostly on account of his good looks. André is a handsome hero. He has his father's drive, his lithe physique, the line of his shoulders and hips, something that, more than twenty years later, still affects the ageing woman she has become. André's beauty is something for which Gabrielle feels responsible; it involves her, while the rich parade of his heroic virtues, made manifest and celebrated by the times, is something of only very distant interest to her. Neither she, nor Paul Lachalme for that matter, has had any part in that. Gabrielle is smoking a small aromatic cigar; it is her Sunday evening ritual; for a few months now, she has permitted herself this male pleasure late in the day, despite her previous fear of the well-recognised consequences for breath, teeth and skin. She is nestled into the soft hollow of her old green armchair, plumes of smoke float about her, her son is a hero, she thinks, his father in hiding. It is something she has only recently discovered, by way of a one-time neighbour, a clerk at the Palais de Justice courts whom she ran into last Saturday on the bus. Sanctimonious and simple-natured, Germaine, a plump and voluble widow, had lived in the same building as Gabrielle, on rue Victor-Chevreuil in the twelfth arrondissement, for ten years, from

1928 to 1938. Gabrielle has perfect recall when it comes to dates: widowed in August 1927 and childless, Germaine had moved out three weeks before she herself had, in July 1938. The law courts had been her home, she was happy to recount the intrigues, her daily source of oxygen, not without vim and vigour and with a slightly precious air of exaggeration that had remained unaltered through the war's long interlude. Gabrielle knows how to keep a secret; in ten years of amicable relations between neighbours, she had never told Germaine what Paul Lachalme meant to her, that high profile lawyer in the 1930s, whose name would often crop up in the multitudes of chronicles from the Palais which were exchanged between the two women every week, on a Saturday or Sunday, over a coffee and cigarette. Germaine found Gabrielle fabulously alluring and Gabrielle loved Germaine's regular information bulletins. Gabrielle settles into her armchair which is illuminated by the soft yellow halo of a thin standard lamp topped by an oversized floral shade. Germaine could not have known that this Gabrielle, whose freedom and spark she used to envy, had been listening out in her pre-war stories for the muffled echoes of a long party to which she had not been invited. Their chance reunion has prompted in Gabrielle an unexpected emotion. Germaine had not changed, apparently frozen for more than fifteen years at some indeterminate age, something close to sixty, an age that Gabrielle with some reluctance now found herself approaching; it was noticeable, it was starting to be noticeable. Gabrielle had sensed in Germaine's grey gaze a hint of bemusement combined with shock. She, Gabrielle, was coming undone. The war years had been harsh and abrasive. Men no longer saw her; it had happened little by little and there would be no let up. A second little cigar was in order, and perhaps even a drop of that plum eau-de-vie she had brought back from Figeac at the end of August. Now, Germaine had said nothing, but her look had been enough to allow Gabrielle to gauge the extent of the damage. Worn, frayed, tired out, the conquering Gabrielle, about whom Germaine knew more or less nothing, and certainly not that she was hiding a son in the Lot who was the result of her previous and passionate amorous relations with Paul Lachalme. The bedazzled court clerk used to repeat at every possible opportunity that the young lawyer would have made the ideal son-in-law; had she had a daughter, that's the sort of man she would have wanted to see her marrying. Gabrielle had not sought to undermine the foundations of this matrimonial predilection which was all the more incongruous given that Paul Lachalme, a committed and notorious polygamist, would, on the available evidence, have made a deplorable husband. For more than ten years she had relished the singular and stupefying happenstance that had led to her having a respectable enough neighbour who lived across the landing and was familiar with the existence, habits, customs, practices and minor exploits and caprices of her

most ardent lover, a first-rate phantom and the vanished
father of André, her secret son.

The eau-de-vie and lingering cigar are good company
and Gabrielle recognises the same pleasure, not felt since
1939, at having had a head start on the prattling Germaine.
A week after their chance meeting on the bus, they had
met up once again, just the previous evening, in a sleepy
café on boulevard Voltaire where Germaine had, with no
further encouragement, resumed her gossiping where she
had left off. She had not been reticent about the fact that
not everything bore repeating and that one had to know
when to turn a blind eye, or simply wipe the slate clean;
she had waggled her head, grown a little flustered, had
stirred her spoon in her now cold milky tea; not that she
had always been comfortable with it, far from it, but one
had to earn a living, even if it meant riding out the storm.
Germaine's expressions, which Gabrielle did not recognise
as the woman's own, wiping slates, riding out storms, blind
eyes, were doing a poor job of concealing a sort of tepid and
sticky discomfort which had, little by little, dissipated over
the course of the conversation, even if Gabrielle was not
certain she followed Germaine's every rambling digression.
She had allowed to wash over her the flood of concerns
related to the murky circumstances of the Occupation and
Liberation that Germaine appeared to place on a strict
equal footing in her account. Gabrielle's attention had wan-
dered and she had waited for the moment to interject with

an apparently innocuous question about the most brilliant
pre-war lawyers, how they had managed, how they had
navigated various dangerous turns. Germaine was ahead
of her; Gabrielle was bound to remember Paul Lachalme,
their darling from their time in rue Victor-Chevreuil; the
question called for nothing more than a hasty acknowledge-
ment, deliberately nonchalant. Paul Lachalme had made bad
choices, and had placed his bets on some sorry nags; he had
compromised himself and had not been seen at the Palais
since the spring of 1944; he had been neither prosecuted nor
disbarred, but nothing more had been heard of him; there
had been rumblings, there were still rumblings, vague and
persistent rumours. Germaine had pursed her lips. She did
not quite understand how or why a boy, a man, she had
corrected herself, a man of such calibre could have lacked a
nose for what was happening to that extent. He had behaved
no worse than many others, but he had not felt the wind
change and had carried on for too long without protecting
his back; that was how the horses had come in, such was
Germaine's final and categoric expression, Paul Lachalme
was trying to lie low in Sologne, where he was said to have
various family connections. Gabrielle had heard enough and
was not sure she would resume an ongoing relationship with
Germaine. She was fond of her solitude, had never really
had any female friends, and did not seek out the company
of other women who in turn found her annoying when
they were not upset by her. Germaine had shown herself

to be all the more relaxed since finding herself without a husband and thus no longer threatened on the marital front. Deep down, and Gabrielle found herself unable to ignore the evidence, notwithstanding the cigar and eau-de-vie, she had become more or less indifferent towards Paul Lachalme, and Germaine was no longer of any interest to her. She was growing older, she was letting things go. Paul Lachalme would also age, and poorly; she knew him well enough to know that he would emerge from his Sologne retreat bitter and contemptuous, armed with his store of bad faith and his formidable self-assurance. Yet, times had changed. Youthful arrogance was no longer appropriate, Paul Lachalme would have to tone it down, not an area in which he showed any aptitude and not one for which he had been prepared.

Gabrielle stands up, empties the ashtray, washes it carefully and takes her time rinsing her liqueur glass. Her small apartment is at once bare and cosy, she could stay here forever. Forty square metres where she will meet no opposition, suffer no disappointment, no betrayal. She makes every decision. Each item has its place, and remains there, the ashtray and the glass from the liqueur service will be put back where they belong. In the yellow kitchen, Gabrielle leans her forehead against the cold windowpane; nobody in the street, everyone is at home, with their families. In this regard, Gabrielle harbours not a single regret; no family except for the distant and benevolent Hélène and Léon, even if from time to time she feels herself the subject of surges of disapproving suspicion from Léon, which he suppresses so as not to upset his Hélène. The sparkling company of her nieces, when they were children, would distract her from the heavy boredom of her stays in the Lot but now she has nothing to say to the bustling wives and mothers they have become, even if the eldest and the youngest are nurses, as she had been in her previous life, before her departure for Paris. She no longer understands why, at the age of eighteen, she had been so keen to pursue a career for which she had no aptitude. Paris had been a deliverance; people did not know who she was, she was not being judged, not being assessed. Courtesy of some vague relation in Aurillac, she had managed to find a secretarial position at a wholesaler of wine and fine foods located in the twelfth arrondissement, where her organisational skills, her liveliness, and her methodical habits had worked wonders. Her boss had been fond of her; he hailed from Laroquebrou himself and had a tendency to take under his wing all the natives from the Cantal and its neighbouring regions. She had been fortunate, and had that been all that was involved in making the great leap to the capital, she would have been better off to have made it far sooner. She had had to cross paths with Paul Lachalme in the infirmary at the Aurillac lycée for boys in order for her to dare take the plunge. That was her only regret and she preferred not to wonder what her life would have looked like had she found her way to Paris at the age of eighteen or twenty. Gabrielle hears footsteps on the stairs; it is the neighbours returning from Cormeilles-en-Parisis where they spend every Sunday with the whole family. They have three children, brown-haired boys, cheerful and rambunctious, who squabble on the landing. She has always excelled in maintaining easy neighbourly relations that do not give rise to any sense of obligation, provided one keeps the right distance, as with Germaine. Gabrielle knows how to keep her distance, with neighbours and with family; with men, it was another matter, a matter now conjugated in the past. André's very existence results from a poor appreciation of distance when it comes to men. She cannot now recall the exact name of the defect that affects her vision and led to her abandoning any attempt to pass her driver's licence. That is another source of regret; she has always envied men in this respect and she knows well enough that young women are also starting to get their licences, and not just in the city, two of her three nieces are already driving. Perhaps she was born ahead of her time. She gives herself a shake in the tiny pink perfumed bathroom. She still gets an excellent night's sleep. They would be consigned to the oblivion of the night, all of them, Germaine, Paul Lachalme, drivers' licences, Resistance heroes, and the skiver in Sologne. Tomorrow is another day.

Thursday, 8 November 1984

WE'VE REACHED SAFE HARBOUR, a blessed safe harbour. They are Léon's words, his voice, that rush to the surface in André's memory when at last they arrive in Chanterelle and disembark in the square in front of the church. That is what Léon would have said, stretching his arms and legs in a deliberate fashion when he emerged from the car. They have brought Hélène with them, suggested they take a trip to the Cantal, and extracted her from Figeac, a place haunted by Léon's death. She has always been fond of a car trip, being driven about, commenting on the countryside, the style of the houses, and what one can imagine of people's lives. Léon had fallen short of a glorious century by two brief years and Hélène, whom nobody considers mortal, is giving him a run for his money. Gabrielle and Léon suffered the same death, in the same house, his ten years after hers, and within two days of each other, August 14 and 16, 1974 for her and 1984 for him. Two clean deaths, no messing around. They took their leave in their sleep, one morning they did not wake up. Hélène found them. Hélène again who keeps saying that Léon was still warm and supple; it had taken her a while to realise, he was lying next to her, on her right, and he was lost, so far away, gone, she had lost him. They were the words Hélène had used, two days after the funeral, to Juliette and André who had remained with her and would only return to Toulouse the following Sunday. She had also spoken about Gabrielle and her efficient death, on site, at home, with none of the complications a Parisian death would have entailed; they had smiled, all three of them, at that word, efficient, which Hélène had emphasised, repeating, your mother was like that, efficient to the end, and you take after her. André did not know how he took after his mother and thought very little about her, dead or alive, but he and Juliette had often wondered how Hélène and Léon had been able, their entire lives, to display such magnanimity and generosity towards a woman who had tricked them into having a fourth child. He had started thinking about it in this way when he turned fifty and had always felt it to be doubly correct. Hélène and Léon had been duped into having him, the cherished and cosseted additional child, and Paul Lachalme too, had probably been duped, the man who had had no room for him in his life, who could not have, would not have known how, would not have wanted to make room for him. Chanterelle wears its old-fashioned kingdom's name in curious fashion. A vast sky wheels overhead in the golden light of an interminable

Indian summer. Chanterelle is empty, desperately blue, besieged by light. Hélène and Juliette make their way over to the church. André remains leaning against the boot of the car for a few minutes. All this blue is making him dizzy. This is his father's hilltop territory, where his father was born and grew up; all of a sudden he understands how Léon's death has changed everything; Léon has vacated this place, his place, and has left him defenceless, depleted, to the point where at last he feels he must head up to Chanterelle, somewhere he has known about for almost forty years without ever having tried to find out what it looked like or understand where Paul Lachalme came from. Chanterelle was his father's own fort; that much is at once evident upon seeing the double-fronted building that takes up the left-hand side of the square and looks across to the Mairie, itself a building of more modest proportions next to a smart-looking general store on its right. The sign, *À La Providence, Maison Lachalme et fils*, has not been removed and remains quite legible on the facade of the prouder of the two buildings, which is also the most recent. The three car doors slammed in the warm silence. It is not yet half past two. They took lunch in Riom-ès-Montagnes, supposedly less sleepy than Condat where Hélène, who still has a healthy appetite, was concerned they would not find a decent meal. André and Juliette have all the time in the world, they have both been retired since 8 October, a month ago to the day; they retired together, Juliette having brought hers forward to match André's timing. In mid-December they will join Antoine who has been living in Canada for the last six months and is talking about settling there; they will spend the festive season there, do some sightseeing, they will visit Chicago, too, and New York and will only return at the end of January. Autumn will be spent with Hélène who needs them, even if she is doing her best to cope and still has her pride. They are comfortable together, the three of them; they get along without the need to speak, and they share an easy understanding amongst themselves. Hélène says they make a good team. Now it's a matter of seizing the moment, and not waiting for something irrevocable to interrupt their momentum. The Cantal adventure had been decided upon two days earlier; areas south of the Loire, and across the entire Massif Central in particular, were experiencing an extended Indian summer, the horsey-looking weather lady had confidently declared. What if we were to head up to take a little look around Chanterelle, Juliette had said. André had thought that at this time of year the bird would no longer be in its nest, on the assumption he were still alive and continued to spend his winters in Paris, as was open to supposition. In fact, he had not supposed much at all for twenty-two years, and the 1962 expedition at Easter time had allowed a layer of controlled indifference to settle over things, lending them an acceptable form. André takes stock; a distant and intermittent mother, that much was true, and a phantom father; but he had had Hélène, Léon, his cousins, the house and garden and the whole of rue Bergandine with its plane trees, and he had had Juliette and Antoine. He had grown into a man, after the high times of the maquis, with that peacefulness, that courage, that spirit, with the zest for life that had characterised his whole childhood and not deserted him, not yet, at more than sixty years of age. On the very evening of Léon's death, he and Juliette had been thinking about words from their younger years; they had remembered the Padirac Chasm and the words uttered by Gabrielle on their wedding day. Gabrielle had been dead for ten years; there was a statute of limitations on her silences, her grand airs, her bouts of disdain and that grenade whose pin she had pulled, to no avail, at the very wedding table of her son. Something that might be characterised as benevolence, over which this family seemed to hold a perpetual monopoly, had nipped in the bud the Parisienne's capacity to do harm.

Thirty-five years later, without incident or bloodshed, André, Juliette and Hélène are in Chanterelle, standing before a building whose faded render and twenty-two pairs of carefully varnished shutters are evidence enough of the costly second residence inherited by beneficiaries who are struggling a little to maintain their inheritance. They imagined there must be a plot of land behind the house and took themselves off to find it with slow steps under the sun's soft touch. Grey stone walls that had seen the recent addition of a dark green wire fence enclosed a rectangle of lawn sloping gently to the stream that ran through the village; the Lemmet, a tributary of the Santoire, which flows into the Rhue at Condat, declared Juliette who had always had a passion for proper nouns and insignificant matters hidden away in small corners of overlooked parts of the world. The general store would be open at three o'clock, the church was closed, but the recently spruced-up cemetery on the side of the hill, flooded with russet, almost sparkling light caught the eye; names, dates, life spans one could not help but calculate, a few commanding family vaults rising with assurance amid graves that lay listless in the air's irreverent warmth. Juliette was the first to pause before a dark vault inscribed with golden lettering which set out André's complete paternal genealogy; a profusion of Lachalmes, and wives with maiden names of Fourgoux, Santoire or Combes. No photographs, nor scrolled plaques, just family names, first names, dates and two enormous, gleaming white chrysanthemums that would be devoured by the first frost. Ever the diligent gardener, André resisted an instinctive gesture which would have had him poking the soil in the pots to check if the flowers needed watering. He caught Juliette's gaze. Hélène's voice was growing louder, she was listing first names, family names, dates. André and Juliette had already taken it all in with a look. Paul Lachalme was only eighty-one years old, he may not be dead, and, if he were, he may not have been buried in Chanterelle. Hélène was calculating aloud, André said nothing; Georges Lachalme,

1905–1983, probably a brother; and the most recent to be interred in the vault; Hélène hated vaults, their gaping black mouths, their vertical pride, and the oily oozing she imagined within, the persistent, stagnant seepage. Lucie Lachalme, *née* Santoire, 1883–1960, probably the boys' mother, and Marguerite Santoire, 1886–1963, a spinster sister of the mother who had continued to be associated with the Lachalme household, both Santoire sisters swallowed up by the same Lachalme vault in Chanterelle. Hélène reads out the father's name, too, Guillaume Lachalme, 1865–1935. Armand Lachalme, August 2, 1903–April 28, 1908, a brother and, it was plain, a twin, a third boy and a dented dynasty. The child's dates are specific; they reflect the joy of a summer at the dawn of the century, two firstborn sons, a thirty-eight-year-old man anxious to perpetuate the family name, a young woman of twenty and her seventeen-year-old sister busy with the infants; Juliette imagines the abyss of that 1908 spring, too, the striking down, a childhood illness, she thinks, that must have carried off the less robust of the twins. Every family harbours in their intimate recesses these young deaths that were the lot of the times, a form of tithe extracted from a surfeit of offspring and paid to Lares, the household deities, in fresh and tender flesh. The church bell chimes three o'clock, the air is blue, they are alone in this charming cemetery and Juliette, who has a sense of what she calls her funereal novels, knows that they cannot remain where they are, that they must return to reality, to the here and now. She suggests a visit to the general store which will have opened again; she excels in the art of loosening tongues without ever appearing to insist, to dig around, to snoop. The shop is bright; a rather shy young woman is busy among the shelves; yes, they are welcome to sit down for a drink, they can just go through to the next room, the only café in the village, with a front window that opens onto a short street bathed in sunshine. The young woman is emboldened; it is quiet, she is able to manage the shop in the afternoons on her own, even with the café and the post-office and banking services, she sells bread too, meat and vacuum-packed meals, lightbulbs, sponges, matches; you have to stock a bit of everything to retain those customers who live on their own in the village and who don't drive, or don't drive anymore, and who depend entirely on the *Shopi*. The young woman has dark hair and pale skin; when she says *Shopi* it is obvious she is doing her best and is fond of her business; it's precarious, they started up in May, the local community gave them a hand to do the place up and fit out the van, her husband does deliveries as far away as Puy-de-Dôme, around Mongreleix, Espinchal and La Godivelle, and even further; they want it to work, they were born in the village, both of them were; they've lived for a bit in other places, in Clermont, in Saint-Étienne, but this is where their life is. Juliette listens, nods in agreement; Hélène, too. Juliette embellishes, Chanterelle is such a pretty name, not one you forget. Hélène picks up the thread with

her white lie, my husband, who has just passed away, had
had a friend from his high school days in Aurillac who came
from Chanterelle, his name was Paul, Paul Lachalme. They
had stopped by the cemetery, found the family vault, Juliette
adds, does the name Paul Lachalme mean anything to you,
being from these parts, even if you're too young yourself,
of course. The young woman grows animated, points to
the two buildings on the other side of the square, explains,
a big family around here, they come often, they left again
on October 30 or 31, shut up the house, they're here for a
long time, the whole summer, two months, and they come
back to open up the house at Easter and for All Saints' too.
They're very attached to the place and buy all their bread
and pastries from the shop, as well as cold cuts and stuffed
cabbages. She reconsiders, the name Paul doesn't ring any
bells, he must be the one everybody calls the lawyer, the
brother of the doctor who was buried last winter, a huge
amount of snow that day, the lawyer lives in Paris, he returns
often to the village but doesn't go out much, he spends most
of his time fishing, she knows the young ones better, who
must have just turned forty or so and do all the shopping;
but her grandmother, Suzanne, spent her whole life working
for the grandparents who died a long time ago now, she
lives right over there, behind the church, she's ninety and
still sharp, especially when it comes to anything from the
old days, she'd be able to tell them, about Paul Lachalme
and the rest of the family. The young woman's expression

is regretful, her grandmother would have enjoyed a visit, but she isn't at home, she's in Aurillac until the following day to have her cataracts seen to, they're operating even though she's so old, she couldn't wait any more, she was in too much discomfort. The following Monday, in Toulouse, before going to bed, André will show Juliette a piece of card from his wallet; he has written everything down, family names, first names, dates of births and deaths; and that epitaph, too, that had been inscribed on another gravestone in the cemetery at Chanterelle, the first one immediately to the right on the way in: To my father, Death will deliver us from the secret, Your son.

Monday, 19 August 1974

ANDRÉ WILL ALWAYS BE ten years old under the plane trees in rue Bergandine. It has been forty years since André was ten years old but the exquisite stifling heat, the mottled bark of the trunks, the very hour, the afternoon lull, the date, all of it takes him back to that third week of August and to the afternoon train, the four o'clock train they used to say, which would deliver him from Gabrielle and restore him to a lightness of spirit, to his games, to the summery feel of things. His man's body baulks but childhood stands firm and pain does not take no for an answer. He thinks about the mole, he has not forgotten anything, he has simply lived. Something is starting over again, the film sputters, hiccups. He has had this vertiginous feeling once or twice before, the sensation of walking in old footprints, but never with such clarity. Hélène, Léon and the trio of cousins are there, in the half-light of the still-cool house. The cousins have come alone, just the girls, *en filles,* as they say prettily; Gabrielle was not everybody's cup of tea in the extended family. André tells himself that you probably have to be related by blood to understand and accept the dogged, unfailing devotion nurtured by Hélène and her family when it came to the Parisienne, who would appear and disappear, who was not raising her son, who made a mystery out of everything, and who would laugh shrilly with her three nieces under the wisteria arbour at the bottom of the garden on a summer's evening. André ponders. Blood does not count for anything. Léon is his chosen father, his father-elect; people say the two of them have the same voice and the same intonation to the point where the cousins sometimes are mistaken on the telephone and confuse them. The grey-green of André's eyes, his ocean eyes, Juliette had read that in a novel when they were newly married and the expression had remained between them like a caress, his ocean eyes belonged to Gabrielle, and to Hélène and Claire, the middle cousin, his soul's sister, his *sœur de cœur*. The body accommodates, the body settles. André knows only that one part of himself is missing, has foundered forever with Gabrielle. With Gabrielle, you would chat, you would laugh, you would tell stories about other people's lives, but you would not talk. Nobody had been able to, or had truly known how to, not even Hélène. André leans back for a moment and feels through the white cotton of his shirt the fleshy bark of the familiar plane trees against his skin. Somebody will have to go up to Paris, to take care of the apartment and paperwork, to sort, to empty, to return the keys. His stomach knots. Paris is Gabrielle's territory, a place of ghosts, Paris is a minefield. He does his calculations; over the last twelve years, ever since the Easter of 1962, he has only been back when he has had no choice, three or four times a year, when he has had to for work. He refused, without hesitating, without so much as speaking about it to Juliette, an excellent position which had been offered to him at the new site not far from Orly. He had sensed how his closest colleagues, Christian, Yves, and his superiors had been dumbfounded by this insuperable reluctance when they knew he was not lacking in courage, was ready to adapt to any situation and had a talent for finding the perfect solution to the thorniest of logistical problems. He will go to Paris, with Juliette, they will go, they will take care of everything; it's a job for them, he knows that. Hélène is grieving, he would like to spare her the trips, the process, the tiresome, painful sorting. They would go up perhaps with Léon, whom age has not diminished; they will have to discuss that, this evening, in the cool, in the garden, or tomorrow, or in the next few days. The clock strikes half past five. A Mass was said for Gabrielle because that is the custom; a few hymns had been sung and some tepid prayers mumbled. The sermon was half-hearted, a child of this country, who had remained faithful to her roots, summonsed back by the Lord, accompanied to her final resting place by her family. The usual litany of clichés had washed over André, he had not prayed, he does not pray; to what, to whom had Gabrielle been faithful, to herself, to her own pleasures, to her secrets? The three cousins are also upset, but not like Hélène, not in the same way. When they were younger, even as children, they had loved this aunt, perfumed and made-up, their father would say "dolled up"; Gabrielle knew how to select the perfect little gifts for them, cheap jewellery, Eau de Cologne in a pretty vaporiser, sparkly belts, and how to lend them a more precious allure with two rustling leaves of tissue paper and a glossy ribbon. They had loved her squeals of delight that only they knew how to elicit and share under the arbour. Despite the neighbours' knowing looks and avid expressions, they had loved her breeziness, the freedom they had never judged, ever, not even later, when they became wives and mothers, even when confronted with the unanimous perplexity of their three husbands. André was the key to everything; no Gabrielle, no André, the Parisienne's most beautiful gift, her masterpiece, André, who had bewitched them for a whole decade of their lives, the second one, ten years that would forever be filled with light.

The apartment smells of stale absence. They had climbed a pleasant, sparkling clean staircase, up to the third floor. André's only thought on locating the building on rue de la Roquette was that it was much less well-to-do than boulevard Arago. Twelve years later, the image had resurfaced, striking and precise, of an elegant facade, with only subtle embellishments. Parisian stone, poor man's dressed stone, Léon announced, as if he could read André's every thought.

Imitating Hélène's actions, they opened the five windows onto the internal courtyard to a majestic chestnut tree, round and lush, russet and glorious in the autumnal light. Gabrielle would always comment that it was very quiet, that she would sleep with the window open from April through to October; Hélène's voice pitted itself valiantly against the void, holding it at bay. They had feared a degree of untidiness and a sorry accumulation of stuff which might have complicated the task ahead of them. They discovered, to their relief, a sparsely furnished living room and bedroom and, to the left off a tiny entrance hall, a yellow kitchen and adjacent pink bathroom, impeccable, almost monastic. There would perhaps be surprises when they opened the cupboards. Hélène had insisted on coming up to Paris to take care of her sister's affairs, she had not let the matter drop, had insisted. Léon was the only one already familiar with the place; he had come, in August 1938, to settle Gabrielle in, loading his van up with his sister-in-law, her luggage and four or five pieces of furniture, a green armchair, a narrow armoire, a bedside table, a small kitchen cabinet made from blonde wood and a round-bellied chest of drawers which would return to the fold in the Lot. André remembered that August 1938 departure because there had been a break from the railway ritual and considerable debate as to whether he too should be loaded up. At the age of fourteen he could at last get to know the capital, his birth place, and he could also lend a hand to haul the furniture up to the third floor, even if Gabrielle insisted on roping in two friends for that purpose, sturdy, well-built and dedicated. The friends, two nuggety olive-skinned impassive brothers, endowed with strong Italian accents, had only reinforced Léon's conviction that his sister-in-law was a magician of sorts, a sorceress perhaps, in any event, in her own way, a leader of men. These two tomcats dragged in from the gutter, Léon would not refer to them in any other way, had been there, indeed had been very much present, but not André; less than a week prior to departure he had fallen off his bicycle and broken his right arm and collar bone, the boy who in all his fourteen years, could only ever have come off his bike two or three times. There was no fuss made. André would not be going up to Paris in his mother's wake. Thirty-six years later, he was discovering his mother's real life, her traces, the folds of her existence, her very worn green armchair, her bare bedroom, her perfectly organised wardrobe, her two piles of handkerchiefs, tiny, white, monogrammed squares to the right, large blue and green checked men's handkerchiefs to the left, her clothes sorted by colour, dresses, skirts, blouses, coats, jackets and one or two pairs of trousers. Opening both doors of her wardrobe, they had been assailed by the lingering scent of Gabrielle's perfume, enduring, elegant, at once sharp and sweet, and by the careful colour combinations. Later, having returned to Figeac, Hélène would regret not having thought to take a photograph for her daughters as a final piece of evidence of her Parisian sister's hidden talents. They looked for and, without any trouble, found the documents divided into envelopes bearing Gabrielle's large, looping handwriting. Rent, building expenses, electricity, telephone, tax, pension, social security, health, an entire life contained within them, a life now obsolete, the matter closed. The walls were bare, neither crucifix, nor photographs, nor prints or reproductions of paintings, off-white wallpaper, faded but decent, a parquetry floor laid with narrow boards, waxed a thousand times over, that year's firemen's calendar pinned to the cupboard door in the kitchen and, in the third drawer of the chest, in immaculate piles, letters. Gabrielle had sorted them all, must have done so regularly; nothing prior to 1938, as if her life had only started when she had arrived in that flat. Later they would discover under her bed, in her room at rue Bergandine, in Figeac, four rectangular boxes with not a single one missing of the letters sent, twice a month, for close to seventy years, from 1905 to 1974, by Hélène to her older sister, first in Aurillac, then in Paris, at cité de Trévise, rue Victor-Chevreuil and rue de la Roquette. There they were, all of Hélène's letters, arranged according to the year, opened with a letter knife, and also, from within the envelopes, a handful of photographs sent after family celebrations, christenings and springtime Communions that Gabrielle had not attended. The telephone had done nothing to alter the habits of the two sisters who only used it on rare occasions. Gabrielle would reply to Hélène punctually, on the last Sunday of every month, curious, evasive and very meteorological letters; it was grey and cold, or already too hot for April, it had dropped below freezing, it had snowed, three flakes, the damp was creeping into everybody's flats, she was fine, she sent love to each and every one of them, that was her formula, and she would sign off "Gaby", with a dramatic and elaborate flourish which took up a third of the page. Hélène would wait for Gaby's letter, which would arrive in the middle of the first week of the month, and, after reading it out loud at the end of the evening meal, she would slip it into a tall, deep hatbox, monumental and old-fashioned, and inherited from one of Léon's distant cousins, a spectacular woman from Toulouse.

It was plain from rue de la Roquette that the Parisienne had not lived a prosperous life, even if her grand airs might easily have led others to a different conclusion. Perched on the edge of the bed, in the bare bedroom, André had all at once felt very weary, as if overwhelmed by the weight of the silence and the secret that was his lot to bear as a son; an unknown father and a mother who was like a suitcase with a false bottom. This image of the false bottom had come to him there, in Paris, while Juliette, Hélène and Léon were busy in the kitchen organising a bite to eat before launching themselves into the serious business. For the first time, at fifty, he was realising that life in the wings of the maternal stage had been far more austere than one might have been led to believe by the whole summer regalia of a delightedly impulsive Gabrielle, light-hearted, hedonistic even. The flat told another version of the story, one in which Gabrielle would perhaps emerge improved and more distant still. They got stuck into the work of opening up, pulling out, sorting through. The concierge proved very obliging upon being consulted; she used to live in the neighbouring building, had only been looking after number 62 for four years, and had hardly known Gabrielle, whom she called Mademoiselle Léoty. André made certain not to introduce himself as the hidden, provincial son of the said *demoiselle*. In buildings like these where the tenants would steadily grow older, it was common enough to have to dispose of whatever the families did not take away after the death; no unpleasant surprises to worry about with Mademoiselle Léoty, the flat had been well maintained, not like some others, just take the one on the fifth floor, last winter, they were fortunate there had been a particularly cold snap just then, the tenant had been dead in his bed for three days when she had found him; his cat had also died, she avoided using a cruder expression, it must have been dead longer than that, he had laid it out like a mummy in a long metallic box that had been sitting in pride of place on the dining room table, who could imagine that, a man who had looked so well and had climbed those flights to the fifth floor right up to his last day. Hélène and Léon nodded, horrified. People teetered on the edge of the icy chasms of loneliness. André thought his mother had looked after herself well and had exuded efficiency, Hélène's expression came naturally to him, to the point of dying in a convenient place. In the drawer of the bedside table, which Claire would later put in the room of her second daughter Laurence, Hélène found two photographs in a large cream envelope which she handed over to André and Juliette after returning from the cemetery the following All Saints' day; there was no need for any explanations, was all she said, you'll see, André, you'll see. They saw. Back in Toulouse, with the photographs spread out on the kitchen table, beneath the bright pendant lamp, they saw. There he was, the blood father, in pride of place, seated at the far left of the first row in the photograph taken of Terminale I, the 1920–1921 graduating class of the lycée Émile-Duclaux in Aurillac; dark suit and tie, white shirt, legs crossed, left one tossed over the right, left foot elegantly shod, flexed, ankle at right angles, soft, thick hair brushed back, round chin, high forehead. Bodies spoke, hands even more so than the face, long hands, strong yet slender, right hand placed over the left, the fingers of that hand spread starfish-like across the thigh. André was speechless. Juliette said, he was eighteen years old. The second photograph dated from February 1941, Gabrielle had noted on the back, Claire's engagement. André seventeen years old. They recognised Hélène, Léon and Claire grouped together with Claire's two sisters and her fiancé, her fiancé's parents, and André, his features a little blurred, perched on the edge of Hélène's armchair, legs crossed and hands resting together on his thighs, André, revealed as the blatant, patent, ineluctable son of his father.

Friday, 28 April 2008

THE DATES ARE THERE, engraved in golden letters on the dark marble of the vault, almost flashy in the burgeoning April. 2 August 1903–28 April 1908. Armand Lachalme. One hundred years. The day, the month, the year leap out at Antoine. Armand Lachalme died and was buried one hundred years ago, to the day, in Chanterelle, in the Cantal, lofty country, lost country; and he, Antoine, his great-nephew, is hesitating over the precise term to describe the nature of a family relationship of which he has not previously been aware as a soon-to-be fifty-year-old man, so here he is, Antoine Léoty, his great-nephew, a French-American citizen, granted dual nationality more than fifteen years ago, passing through France for three days, between flights, and standing here in front of the grave of this five-year-old child, of whose existence he had known nothing a few hours earlier when he had arrived in Chanterelle behind the wheel of a car rented in Clermont-Ferrand. He is the great-nephew of a five-year-old child, dead and buried one hundred years ago, to the day. He swallows, his palms are moist, suddenly he feels very warm; he has just visited another Armand, Armand Lachalme, born in March 1935, his father's first cousin, nephew of this dead child, and henceforth the sole bearer of the keys to the kingdom of Chanterelle, this afternoon will count for something in his life, he knows it he feels it, it's a switch point a border a threshold. This time the words tumble over each other and he remains standing in the green light that is whisked into curlicues by the sharp breeze, and brushes across the Chanterelle cemetery. Evening will soon come, he is expected in Figeac, at rue Bergandine, a good two hours' drive away; Claire's second daughter, Laurence, lives in the house, she has raised her three children there, she was twelve when he was born but, despite the distance between them, he has enjoyed an enduring and cherished relationship with her, a sort of natural extension, according to his father, of the ties which bound him more to his cousin Claire than to her two sisters. Antoine gives himself a shake, he likes driving, it clarifies his thoughts, but he is struggling to tear himself away from Chanterelle. He stares at the dash on the tomb, the same symbol found under the number six on a French keyboard, an entire life in a dash, a handful of years, barely five, the age of his two sons, twins, Emmet and Enak, who are growing up in Los Angeles, were born in Vancouver, and have already lived in Singapore for two years. Antoine is on a pilgrimage, the word catches him by surprise, in this cemetery, where it has a strange ring, but he finds none better; he tells himself suddenly that the longer he lives and works and thinks in English, the more he is losing his French which is resisting him, baulking and evading him, stultifying and shrivelling; he is on a pilgrimage then, in the footsteps of his father whom he did not see grow old, whom he did not see die. André had not really grown old, he had died all of a sudden, at eighty-five, in his bed, like his two mothers, and like Papa, as Claire used to say, Claire who, at the age of ninety-two, could not get over having had to bury Dadou, so bright, so alert and seven years her junior, Claire who was the only one still to call him that. Laurence and Claire had woken Antoine in Los Angeles where he had just arrived with his wife and children to start a new job. He can see himself there, in the living room, dumbstruck, in the middle of the hardly unpacked boxes; France, Toulouse, Figeac, Claire's voice, Laurence's, another time and place, his own life's beginnings. He had hastened to take a flight to Paris, another to Toulouse, he had come, they had waited for him. He had been there, dazed, at Figeac, at the church and next to the grave, in the warmth of a March afternoon, with the whole tribe from rue Bergandine gathered around Claire, and the friends who had been able to come from Toulouse or elsewhere; his parents were dead, their friends, or those who remained, were old, slow, shrunken, barely recognisable, he felt like a stranger, exposed and undone, in spite of Laurence and Claire. Back home, he had been relieved to be back in a youthful, vibrant world;

he had allowed himself to be caught up and had devoted all his energy to coping with everything, to adapting, reinventing himself in a new environment, after Singapore and before some other city, some other country perhaps, another challenge. Amy, whom he had met in Canada, excelled at making herself at home anywhere; within a few weeks she was already smoothing the edges of the nest she had created for him and the children out of a house that was still new but felt instantly familiar. More than a year had passed, there had been no issues with the estate, André having put all his affairs in order after Juliette's death; Antoine had rarely thought about his father, more about his mother, often dreaming about her, as he had seen her for the last time, at Christmas in 2004, in Laurence's home, translucent, whittled away by her illness, curiously serene and already a little absent, on her way, and yet moved to see, to touch, her two grandsons, her American twins. For almost twenty years, from the time they retired to when his mother first fell ill, his parents had travelled in their wake, spending more than two months a year with him and Amy and then with Emma, over the festive season and then in August. They were not burdensome; curious, dumbfounded sometimes, never derisive or scornful, they were so easily delighted and remained intrigued by the world and madly besotted with their three grandchildren, the eldest of whom, Emma, owed them her basic, but effective, singsong French.

Antoine thinks of Amy who will want to understand

everything, will ask questions, tally dates, with that peculiar
passion for genealogies which she gets from her mother-
in-law. He takes a photograph of the vault at Chanterelle,
of·Armand's dates, those of Paul Lachalme, 1903–1998,
the hardened forebear, the surviving twin, the absent one,
his grandfather by blood, he takes one of Georges' dates
too, the next born, progenitor of the official family line,
who was born in 1905 and died in 1983. Antoine recaps,
mentally files, classifies; a little overcome, he tries to get
his bearings. Paul Lachalme was his grandfather, even if
that position will really continue to be occupied by Léon,
Georges was his great-uncle, and he has just spent more
than three, almost four, extraordinary hours with his son,
Armand Lachalme, born in 1935, nephew and godson of
Paul Lachalme, time that to him felt as if he were in a sort
of peaceful and profoundly moving trance, walking in his
father's footsteps, daring to go where André never would,
never could. Antoine feels it weighing on him, churning
him up, feels the shifting of tectonic plates; he wishes he
had better defences, he feels he could start to weep right
there, in the green Chanterelle evening, next to the grave of
this child whose death is undiminished. After two hours of
nibbles and preliminary conversation spent exclaiming over
the few mementos Antoine had brought with him, and a
family album exhumed from a crammed bookcase, Armand,
caught by surprise as he was busy gardening but quickly
amenable and chatty, had explained the burden of his first

name, which had fallen to him in memory of a maternal uncle killed at the age of twenty-two at Les Éparges and of the child who had been martyred in that very house in April 1908. He had used the word martyred several times, before pointing out that it was the family's word; Lucie, the grandmother, and her sister, Marguerite, who had always lived with her, his uncle and godfather Paul, and even his father, Georges, had never used any other. Armand had not died, he had been martyred, scalded, on a household laundry day, by a maid, whose name, Antoinette, had of course astounded Antoine. The dreadful story had been passed down over a century and Armand told it with a muted emotion, in short, controlled phrases that Antoine would never forget. The father had moved heaven and earth; the doctor from Allanche, who had come as fast as he could on horseback, had sought assistance from a colleague in Aurillac, to no avail; all the women in the village had prayed, night and day, the mother and aunt had never left the child, swaddled in bandages soaked in greasy ointment; Armand had held on from Thursday until the Sunday; at dawn he had stopped moaning and, through the silence that settled back over the house had come the howling cries of the father who, for three days, had neither closed an eye, nor eaten, nor drunk. Antoinette had been twenty years old, had just married and left the house where she only now returned to help out on the busy days when there was much work to be done, she had been expecting her first child, she adored Armand who had cried so much when she had left. For Antoinette it had marked the beginning of her misfortunes which had seen no end. She had gone mad, to the point where she had been unable to look at her own daughter, born the following autumn; she had stopped speaking, would only moan or scream, would refuse to wash or to drink, would disappear, running barefoot down the road back towards Chanterelle, where she had lived until her wedding day and where in fact she had been buried. Her husband and parents had to have her committed in Aurillac, where she had died ten years later, in 1918. Antoine even knows where Antoinette's grave is, opposite the Lachalme vault, he would only have to retrace his steps; Armand had told him as much, adding that, since the death of his wife, he avoided visiting cemeteries, especially in the evening, so he would not accompany him back to the one in Chanterelle, which was nonetheless worth a visit for its charming setting with that marvellous aspect, so beautifully maintained by the local municipality.

Antoine could weep in the Chanterelle cemetery, but he will not; not yet, not now, not all alone, not this time. He has to be on his way, Laurence is expecting him; tomorrow he will return the rental car to the airport in Toulouse, take a plane back to Paris and on to Los Angeles, winding up a work trip from which he had been able to extract, at Amy's tenacious instigation, two days dedicated, reserved, devoted, he hesitates over the choice of words, to fathers, to absent fathers, to their silences, their secrets. In thirty-six hours' time, he will have returned home, he will see Emma and the boys again, their laughter, their racket, and Amy who will listen to him. He makes notes, he takes photographs, this evening he will speak with Laurence, then Amy will help him, together they will set things straight; she will sketch out a family tree on the back of an envelope and everything will fall into place, she will have the patience. She is going to love the photographs of the house and of Armand Lachalme, the one who is alive, very much alive and well, the one born in 1935; he kept Chanterelle, out of fondness and enthusiasm, his sister Pauline having been happy to relinquish it to him. Amy is going to love Armand's keen face, his straw hat, his flowerbeds, what he calls his priest's garden, and what he has done, what they have done, he and his wife, with this impossible enormous consuming pile, sitting there in Chanterelle, Cantal, Auvergne, France. Antoine realised that Armand had been widowed for a number of years; he saw the photographs, on the living room mantelpiece, of a dark-haired, slender woman; no evidence of any children, or grandchildren, but nothing specific was said and he did not dare to ask any questions. Antoine likes Armand and Amy would like him, will like him, too; he senses it, another family history could start with this abiding and well-honed Armand who did not for a second hesitate to acknowledge the physical evidence, between Paul Lachalme and André Léoty, in the photographs extracted from Gabrielle's big cream envelope. The mere name Chanterelle has been enough to have Amy dreaming ever since she first heard it; she used to tell André and Juliette that Chanterelle had to be an enchanted kingdom, a place of magic and miracles. André, out of love for his romantic and only daughter-in-law, would smile, remain evasive, move on to other things; Juliette would tell them, would explain, as much as they knew, what they could never know, what Hélène had said, what she had not said, or had not known, or had not wanted to know, along with the lost secrets of Gabrielle, whom Amy of course had not known and whom Antoine himself only barely remembered, having been only fourteen when she died. He had never, for that matter, been surprised by the fleeting presence at Hélène's side of this Parisian sister, long and stiff, whom he knew to be his father's mother but not really his grandmother. Juliette, when she fell ill, had bequeathed to Amy what she used to call the relics from the Padirac Chasm; the crossed correspondence, Juliette loved that expression, exchanged between the two sisters had remained at rue Bergandine, when it became Laurence's home, but Amy had slipped a third photograph into Gabrielle's precious cream envelope, the one dated Saturday, 21 April 1962 on the back, in Juliette's hand, of André standing valiantly in front of the building at 34 boulevard Arago, along with the note drawn up after the visit to the Chanterelle cemetery on 8 November 1984. Antoine ruminates; 1962, 1984, 1998, a whole life spent hunting for the trace of a father, from a distance or up close, in Paris or in the Lot; fourteen years between that inaugural visit to Chanterelle, which Juliette had been happy to talk about, and Paul Lachalme's death, at ninety-five; Laurence would point this out at breakfast the next morning, nothing had been possible despite the extraordinary longevity that Paul Lachalme had unwittingly shared with Hélène, Léon and Claire. Antoine has known for a long time, something had held his father at bay, prevented him from returning to the source up in Chanterelle, something more powerful than the yearning or the absence. His father had known that yearning, had felt that absence. He reflects, he is driving through the cool night, windows down, the exuberant green of the new foliage exploding in the headlights, the high country and its ash trees still bare behind him, he has passed through Aurillac, is rapidly approaching Maurs, Figeac is little more than an hour away. His father had a good life, full and generous, his father was a splendid and fair man, a hero at twenty, nobody is better placed to acknowledge it than Antoine. He can hear the voice of Armand Lachalme, elegant and concise; my uncle had some difficult years after the war, he had to keep his head down, keep a bit of a low profile, which was not his style, my mother and he were like cat and dog, right from the beginning, and my father found himself torn and quartered, he had hesitated before using the words, by the two of them. It was evident that Paul

Lachalme had not left a strong impression on his nephew and godson who had had to divide up between himself and his uncle the Chanterelle properties that were still held in joint tenancies following the death of Georges, the younger brother who had always been ready to submit to the whims of his elder sibling. The whims, Armand said, and repeated, his whims, some of them minor, some of them substantial, along with the habits of an aged spoiled child, hot baths and pears in syrup, a confirmed bachelor and relentless philanderer who had died with no acknowledged offspring. Antoine can still see Armand's smile, the lively gestures of his hands, and his kindness; his father, his mother too, and Hélène, would all have liked the cousin from Chanterelle; cousin Armand from Chanterelle is a fine addition, he has a pleasant way about him and knows how to behave, that's what André would have said, his expressions and voice resurfacing inside the car. Tomorrow morning, Antoine will go to the cemetery with Laurence, they will stand in front of his parents' grave, both of them, the one next to the other. Then Laurence will leave him on his own, she will head off down the empty paths looking, as she always does, as if she is just taking a walk, and she will wait for him. Antoine will talk to his father, and to his mother; even from the other side of the world, in an attempt not to lose touch, he sometimes speaks to his dead, to his mother especially. He will confirm to his father what he already knew, that Chanterelle is a hilltop kingdom stronghold, where the trees are dense and the view is long; he will tell him too that from now on, in Chanterelle, it is known that André Léoty, son of Paul Lachalme and Gabrielle Léoty, existed in this world, and that he will be remembered.